And the

Night Did

Claim Them

First published in Great Britain in 2022 by Black Shuck Books

Cover design by WHITEspace
from "Boy Drinking"
by Annibale Carracci
Courtesy of the Cleveland Museum of Art

Set in Caslon by WHITEspace
www.white-space.uk

978-1-913038-72-4

And the Night Did Claim Them

by
Duncan P Bradshaw

BLACK
SHUCK
BOOKS

One

17th August 1995

For the briefest of moments, we are delivered into the smothering darkness. There's no road. No xylophones being hammered like flayed ribcages to summon the dead from their graves. As the blackness stops contracting and propels us from its cloying, soundless vulva back down that tedious country lane, I hear someone scream a warning, too late for me to react. We strike something and the world lurches violently as time itself grinds to a halt. Paul's feral howl morphs into two words: "Watch it!"

Two

I'm released from the embrace of the night and feel one hand resting on the handle of a beer pump. There's an amber haze in front of me and my fingers are cold and wet. My vision swirls back into focus and I push my hand up instinctively, stopping the flow. I stare at the pint, long since filled to the brim, my fingers shiny from the overspill. Beyond them is Paul's face, a twist of annoyance and resignation. "Sorry," I offer, "I was miles away."

"How about waking up a bit, yeah? Jesus… the drip tray looks like Niagara Falls."

The man's a prick, but he has a point. John'll have my guts for garters if he sees I've wasted this much beer.

The stragglers left in the pub look over at me. Neil shakes his head. "Sacrilege to spill booze, you know." His fat fingers are curled round his glass, near empty. Been pacing his drinking for the last few hours, no doubt, clinging onto the forlorn hope of a little bit of extra time in here. Jen's perched next to him, nursing a vodka and tonic, pushing the glass round the bar top as if she's practising her chess moves, a far-away look on her face.

After letting out a half-inch at the top of Paul's glass, I fill it up so there's at least something of a head on it and set it down. He has the cash ready for me, having raided the shrapnel from his pocket. He places the coins in the palm of my hand, arranged in order of size. At first, I think he's offering me a miniature trophy, a mix of copper and silver. I ruin his arrangement and chuck the money into the till. With the exchange made, he sups from the top, slurping the foam up as he always does, before trotting back to his usual table – the one behind the front door, where coats that should've found a new home in the lost-and-found hang from wobbly pegs.

After drying my hand on a spare towel, which I then chuck onto the floor to soak up the puddle of beer, I resume watch from my stool, nestled into the corner of the bar. Bags of nuts and pork scratchings hang behind me, preventing me from being able to rest against the wall. Seems nothing wants me to get too comfortable tonight.

The pause allows me to consider what's just happened. What the hell was that? I love a good daydream as much as the next guy, but most tend to be a little lighter in tone. Even my jaded outlook on life tends not to get in the way of a little escapism. Was it a portent? A premonition of what will happen if I stay in this job for too long? *Shape up or ship out*, Mum used to warn me. *You treat this house like a hotel* was a common refrain, repeated so often that if it were a recording, the tape would have worn out by now. I always believed that your childhood home was supposed to be a place of nurture and support, not hard-nosed cynicism and cold detachment. When did I stop being her child and start being classified as a tenant? And even then, I wasn't what she'd advertised for; rather I was the one she'd been lumbered with – and whose background checks had come back far

7

from ideal. It made no difference what I said or did, or whichever new rules she introduced and I adhered to, the shipping-out part was always set in stone.

When I came back to see her the first time after I'd moved out, the carpet in my old room had barely had a chance to breathe before it was pulled up and thrown onto the tip, my memories and leavings removed, the room scrubbed clean and painted over. "It's a spare room now," she said, with no hint of irony.

The changes keep on coming; now I've flown the nest, my status is no longer 'domiciled offspring' or even 'guest'. To family and neighbours, I've been granted the honorary title of 'surviving in the real world', each word laden with as much sarcasm as could be mustered. The cherry on top of this shit-cake was delivered aptly during dessert the first time I visited after moving out. After I commented on the speed at which my old room had been repurposed, she pointed to a piss-stained, fold-up camp bed in the corner of the room, telling me flatly that it's the best she could offer should everything go south. And, let's be honest, it's likely to. I left college two years ago and have jacked in four jobs already.

Mum loved that, of course. Each report of my failing to see things through and apply myself tallied up with what she'd been warning me (and anyone who'd listen) for years. "Fail to prepare, prepare to fail," and other such fake Taoisms. Thing is, though, I could always stomach listening to them over the alternative, her well-honed maternal disapproving sigh, able to render any magnificent achievement from marble into slurry. How the hell can a simple exhalation of air conjure up such dread? I don't know how she manages it, but it's certainly a skill. It even travels well by telephone; reporting my A-level results to her when she was at work must've melted the exchange. I can imagine the poor technician trying to work out what had happened, and getting that doleful sigh replayed on a loop until the end of days.

I check the clock: a couple of minutes to eleven. If I'm lucky, I'll get to ring the bell in a bit, then get in the trenches for the final bout of furious pint-pulling when this lot realise that their last chance for booze tonight is nearly up. There's only one thing can stop that from happening, and unless John is going to phone down from his ivory fucking tower, then I'm all good.

"You going to empty this or what?" Neil has his glass halfway to his gob, the bottom pointing accusingly at the ashtray. Every single night, he starts off on his path to getting pissed with bottles of Hooch. After peeling off the labels, he rolls up the shavings and packs out one side of the ashtray with them. He knows it drives me potty, a point he takes pride in making as he stubs out another B&H, igniting his little stash of paper boulders in the process, making acrid smoke waft along the bar.

It's best to get the things he moans about done without complaint. If he gets the slightest inkling that something he's done has pissed you off, he stores it in that stupid fat head of his for later. Anything and everything with that bloke. Reckon he does it to bring everyone down to his level. Always trying to find the bad in things. Never happy, never content. It could be the best day of his entire fucking life and he'd still whinge about something or other. After the first few times of getting wound up by it, I found that it's easier to give in than to argue with him.

Teetering off my stool, I carefully pick up the still-smoking ashtray, seeing a folded bit of paper beneath. "This yours?" I ask. No one bothers to look over, let alone answer me. After dousing the smouldering paper embers and chucking the sodden crap in the bin, I set the glass ashtray back down on its scarred little divot on the bar and unfold the note.

Well done, help yourselves to a nightcap. You've done The Dark Horse proud.

"What does it say?" Neil asks.

Absolutely fucking marvellous. Waking from that daydream back to the wonder of *this* has soured my mood and curtailed any desire I had to stay on here after hours. I chuck the note on the bar, pissed off that any hope of getting home before midnight has been well and truly scuppered. "Read it for yourself."

He silently mouths the words; the corners of his mouth turn up when he realises that John's granted him his simple wish. He sinks the dregs of his pint in one, sets it down, and folds the paper in half. "I'll have another, looks like we're going nowhere, love." Jen quits trying to check-mate herself and leans in. Neil doesn't even look at her, just raises his hand. "You're fine for now," he says, tapping his empty glass with dirty fingernails and looking me dead in the eyes. "Chop-chop." As I begin to refill his drink, he thumbs to the windows behind him. "Make sure you close them properly this time, too. Unless you want another little word in your ear from PC Cums-quickly? The boss upstairs would love that, wouldn't he?"

Har-de-fucking-ha. He's got names for everyone else, too. Thinks it's a sure sign of his wit, when all it does is confirm to all and sundry that he's nothing but a vindictive little shit. It's bad enough the way he speaks to his own wife, and she just sits there trying to smile even though her fucking heart must be breaking. Though I doubt there's enough superglue in the world to put that shattered vessel of hers back together again. I put the pint down on the bar, taking the fiver Neil's already holding out for me.

As I pass him the change, there's another voice to my left. "Cheeky little lock-in, is it?" It's Charlie – he's been drinking in this pub as long as I've been around. I remember sitting in what passes for the beer garden when I was a kid, and seeing his face. No word of a lie, he looks *exactly* the same now as he did back then. I'm surprised no pharmaceutical companies have come out here with their botoxed hearts set on bleeding him dry, eager to uncover his secrets of eternal vitality.

After a while, you come to learn that all pubs have a Charlie in them. It's as if the government assigns one to every single bar in the land to keep an eye on us proles, so he can give the powers-that-be an early warning of malcontent. He's the perfect stooge: completely unflappable. Nothing fazes him, knocks him out of his stride or brings him down – and trust me, Neil has tried his bloody hardest to. Though where others have failed to not rise to the bait – me included – Neil's digs and jibes just bounce off Charlie. Every sneer, every snarky comment and barefaced insult are batted back with Charlie's trademark smile, the one that shows off a little glint of gold.

Man, the stories we made up when we were kids, about how he got that golden tooth. The people he must've killed, the things he'd seen and done, we reckoned that the only souvenir he kept from his incredible adventures was that gleaming little peg.

He shakes his glass to get my attention. Always leaves a little band of lager at the bottom. "Got to leave a tip for the washer-woman," is his oft-spouted reason, one that raises a laugh or two, even now. "Same again please, mucker," he winks, and rests against the bar.

His drink is always the same too, a lager top. Confused the hell out of me the first time he asked for it. Every county has its little nuances, and Dorset is no different. "It's like a shandy," he said, when he saw I had no idea what he was asking me for, "but a bit more manly." A centimetre or so at the top of the glass is saved from being filled with lager, and lemonade is added instead. It seemed completely pointless to me, so as I followed his instructions, I asked him why he bothered, getting another Charlie-ism in reply. "Makes it sweet, just like *me*," the last word always delivered with that wink of his.

He fishes a tenner from his back pocket and takes a mouthful as I'm digging through the till. I know he won't want any notes in return; the change returned to him has to be broken down to small denominations ready for his main activity of the evening. After checking his change, he jingles it in his hand as he struts back to the fruit machine, submitting himself to the bells, whistles, and lights once more.

The clock is now bang-on eleven – from a quick glance, it's just the regulars in tonight, all members of the darts team. I brace myself for the inevitable flurry of activity as I toll the bell. "Last orders, ladies and gents."

Three

The lock-in has put Neil in a good mood, i.e. bordering on insufferable. One beneficiary of this change is Jen, as she's been allowed a top-up. She pushes her glass across to me but doesn't make eye contact. Whilst Neil is giving Charlie an earful about the match earlier on, I make hers a double, but only charge him for the single measure so he's none the wiser. She takes a sip and reels slightly at the extra strength before giving me a half-smile, hiding it as soon as her husband looks back at us.

"Good barkeep," comes the unmistakeable voice of the team captain. Dion has the appearance of an army officer from the first world war: eyes that constantly flit from person-to-person, assessing everything and everyone. His moustache bristles as he anticipates the room-temperature beer I'm about to serve him. The guest ales are delivered on the first of every month, and he spends the next few days working his way through each and every one of them, in alphabetical order I should add, scoring each out of ten in five different categories of his own making. He even does a little drawing of the accompanying picture we bolt onto the front of the pumps. Keeps all his notes and sketches in a little pocketbook, which he hides beneath a buttoned shirt pocket. Bet he's got all sorts in there, his entire life journaled and annotated.

He's the embodiment of routine. Not sure if it was drilled into him at basic training or whether it's always been there, but it's often on show. For example, without fail, he will always taste his pint first before accepting or paying for it. He makes this really annoying *cluck* sound too when it goes down his throat just before he decides to approve it – or not. When it's his round, he fetches the money from one of those weird little cloth purses you only saw as a kid, usually owned by an aunt or your nan. They'd pry open the metal clasp with their bony fingers and peer cautiously inside, before rummaging around and chucking you a coin or two. The first time Dion dug it out of his pocket genuinely shocked me – it was such a stark contrast to the rest of his outward demeanour that if it were anyone else, you'd have thought he'd nicked it. Most people create a façade to cope with the outside world, to stop people from getting in too close, or from finding a corner of the veneer they can pick and tear at just to watch the whole thing unravel. But Dion has employed this well-kempt persona of his for so long now that I'd wager if it were ever threatened, he'd take everyone down with him. Collateral damage. Douse and burn. Never let anyone out alive who discovers the real him, who would dare to dig up the dirty little secrets that were supposed to stay hidden beneath that precise exterior. It comes down to that fear we all share: what if that intruder were to expose your past to everyone you know?

Like most other people, I learned those lessons when I was a nipper. As kids, my brother and I were enrolled without discourse into the popular British school of Not Showing Your Feelings. Daily lessons taught us to keep those pesky feelings we had pushed deep down inside. The mantra was: no matter what happens, no matter what people say or do, never let them out. Ever. It was drummed into us that no-one wants to know how you're feeling, no-one cares, they're a sign of weakness, and rule number one was that there's *nothing* worse than showing people you're weak and vulnerable.

Of course, the minute you stumble out into the big bad world, you discover that all of those lessons were the biggest pile of bullshit you've ever been pelted with. You quickly find out that many of the barriers you've built with your own unresolved neuroses (which you were told would help shield you from the terrors of this world, by the way, good going there!) are more of a hindrance than a help. In time, you realise that the most useful tools you'll ever find are the ones you make yourself from all the life crap you deal with on your own.

You look back on your childhood and see that all your parents did was flood you with their own doctrine, silently congratulating themselves on a job well-done when other people call you a chip off the old block, as if that's any measure of success.

'You've got your father's eyes.'

'Your mother's mind.'

'Your grandad's spirit.'

Whoop-de-woo! Do I get a prize? Yet I'm pretty sure I wasn't born to be a clone of anyone else. I was supposed to find out who I *am*, the things that make me tick, not get a pat on the back when my likeness to some distant relative is pointed out. Problem is, you never find that out in your early twenties, as you're still purging your system of all the crap you've been laden with. Growth requires the true weight of the d to press down on you, to see where you bend and flex. At times, the pressure will be too much and you buckle, and there is no shame in that. Sometimes you have to take it all in so you can let it all out.

All your past is ever meant to be is a guide, never an indelible outline – otherwise, what's the point? If the future is mapped out regardless of how you grow, why bother at all? May as well just strip down to your birthday suit and walk out into the fucking sea. Slap a stamp on your arse and mark yourself *return to sender*. Once the dying bit's out of the way and the pent-up gas has left your decomposing body, your remains can settle into the sediment and provide sustenance to some little critter that'll make better use of you than you ever did. Better that than living your entire life cowering in the shadows of events that you often had no say or control over.

Dion taps his old-woman's purse against the bar, waiting for me to acknowledge him. "Ready?"

"Sorry, what can I get you?"

He points to the optics behind me. "A pint of Gold Hill for me, and a G&T for Mattie, my good man. May as well chuck a packet of Scampi Fries into the bargain too, if it's not too much bother?"

Cheeky sod. Next up comes the delight of the social dance we do with others, figuring out which of us will lead, with which foot, and how much force we should put into every twist and turn. "Single or double?" I know the answer before I've even uttered the words. We all do, yet we still fucking persist with the pointless questions. Every bloody one of us are actors in this elaborate theatrical production of our existence. Just backs up the assertion that everyone is the same beneath this skin and bone, we're so fucking desperate to fit in somewhere with someone, anyone, even it's for a few fleeting seconds.

"Just a single, if you please, don't want to carry her home tonight," he smiles, his lines delivered to perfection without the need for an autocue. I give him the same hollow laugh I've given the last god knows how many fucking times we've done this scene.

I put the drinks and snacks down on the bar, grateful that Dion doesn't open the packet and try *those* before handing the money over. The clasp on the purse clicks open, and he digs around inside for the exact change. For a fleeting moment he's *my* nana, about to ruffle my hair and tell me to spend the money on sweets. Then I take the coins from him, drop them into their rightful place in the till and close the drawer. Slamming it shut signals that the initial flurry is done, time for a moment to myself. Maybe even a chance to fix myself a sneaky pint or—

"Another Guinness, please."

The voice is an unfamiliar one and I look around the bar, trying to pick out the stranger in our midst. Then I find him. He's at the end of the bar, behind a tabletop fountain John picked up from a car boot sale. Said it gave the place a touch of class, but one look around the pub would suggest that none of the ephemera he's picked up has managed to nudge it into that bracket.

The mystery guest is standing in the corner that has been the reserve of the blokes who've been fixing up the High Street for the past few months. They all walk in at five o'clock on the dot, loud and sweaty, drink for two hours straight – as if they're still on the clock – before slurring their goodbyes and staggering off to their restaurant of choice.

John designated that particular section of the bar to be 'one with nature', thinking he'd easily met his own wide-ranging design brief with a job-lot of potted plants from the local garden centre – for which he'd paid half-price, of course. By rights, the bloody things should be dead by now. I don't think anyone waters them, not even the cleaners. Yet somehow, they've thrived. They look like ferns, *small palm trees*, John calls them, but that's definitely pushing artistic license to the max.

I realise I'm still gawping at the man as he takes another pull on his cigarette. "No rush, I've got all the time in the world," he says, not in a sarcastic way, but genuinely. It's as though you could travel to the end of time itself, witness the last sun contract under its own weight and explode into nothingness, delivering the universe into eternal solitude, and he'd still be there, his cigarette cherry the sole source of light in the darkness, an empty glass in front of him, those indestructible, feral, bloody plants his backdrop.

Like seeing Dion's choice of wallet for the first time, I'm struggling to accept that this intruder is in here with *us*. Lock-ins are the reserve of locals – the only time we go against this is if John says it's okay – but judging by the empties this guy has in front of him, he's been here for a few hours at least. I can't remember serving him, but things get a bit hazy around the nine o'clock mark as people flit in and out, ordering either their last one before heading home, or their first on a night out.

I clear the glasses from in front of him, the toffee-coloured foam that coats the inside having dried to a bubbly crust. I fill a fresh glass to the three-quarters mark and let it sit, the black liquid sifting from bottom to top by sheer Irish magic. When I first started here, I made the mistake of pouring it all in one go, and the customer looked at me as if I'd just strangled his firstborn. John stepped in and showed me how it was done, but I've never liked doing it.

It's the waiting, you see. I have zero patience. Never have done – another maternal trait, so I'm told, yet one that's celebrated with little fanfare every time it's on display. I always feel I should be doing something, making the most of every second, even if I'm stuck at work. Still, for once, this delay could work to my advantage. "You from round here?" Another stock line delivered perfectly.

He shakes his head. "Nope, just passing through."

This one's closed tighter than Dion's little flowery purse. I press on. "What do you do?" He looks back at me and takes another pull on his cigarette before tapping the ash into the tray. "For a living, I mean."

"I'm a debt collector."

Click. "Ah." I'm the safe-cracker of people's barriers.

"Yeah … most people aren't too fond of my line of work, so best not to go shouting about it." He taps his nose conspiratorially, then stubs his cigarette out before immediately taking a fresh one from the packet. He rests it between his lips and looks at me, the silence between us yawning like a stretch of midnight asphalt. "Got a light?" Despite the open grave of cigarette butts that is the ashtray, my hand has pulled out my Zippo without even raising the obvious question of how he's managed to spark the others up. Just then, the mental timer in my head dings, and I panic, stuck between two competing tasks. I'm a rabbit dashing from the safety of a hedgerow, caught between the headlights of indecision. I drop the lighter by his packet of Camel

Lights, and turn back to his pint, filling it up to the brim slowly. A lot of bartenders show off by sketching out a four-leaf clover in the foam. Not me, though. For one, I possess the artistic ability of a dustpan and brush, and second, if everyone else does it, it's even less of a reason to do it yourself.

I place the pint in front of him. He's snapped the lighter shut and is examining the pits and marks on the body. Seemingly happy with what he finds, he holds it out to me. I go to retrieve it from his grasp but he responds by applying pressure on his end, so for an instant we're joined together by this hunk of metal. *Flashback to Paul in the minibus.* But there's something *off* with this bloke. His face is a placid caldera, lava bubbling just beneath the surface. Our eyes lock as he takes in a lungful of smoke, before letting it cascade from his lips slowly. He yields his grip. "Much obliged."

"Do I—"

His hand is out before I've finished my sentence. "Simon, pleased to meet ya." My hand is drawn to his, both through conditioned social decorum and the tractor beam his proffered invitation exudes. His fingers close around the top of my hand gently, but the hold is firm. I'm caught in a vice, one that would only bite down harder if I so much as dared to struggle. I guess he's sizing me up, no doubt a common occurrence in his line of work, needing to know who's going to confront him and who is going to accede to his demands. This assessment of his takes less than a few seconds, but I feel as though I've taken root in this grotty corner of the pub.

"Good firm handshake, says a lot about you." With that, he drags across this morning's local paper and starts to go through the half-finished crossword, our initial exchange apparently complete.

"Oi, same again, when you can tear yourself away from your new bum-chum." Neil knocks back his pint and smacks the glass onto the beer mat.

"Yeah, sure." I get back to it; no rest for the wicked, they say, especially not in this place.

Mattie is up next, repaying the earlier favour from Dion. The pair of them go everywhere together, but they're not *together*. The perfect example of a man and a woman being friends and nothing more.

Think they went to school together, and aside from Dion going off to kill people for queen and country a few years back, they're always in the same place at the same time. It's funny how some people are like that. Perfectly complimenting each other, allowing you to do your own thing, but offering enough in return that they want you around too. We know each other, Matilda... *Mattie* and me, but we don't have the same social patter that I have with Dion. Shunning my offer of a tray, Mattie grasps the drinks with her tiny hands and scurries back to their table, before laughing at some story they've undoubtedly shared a hundred times before.

"Aren't you forgetting something?" Neil thumbs behind him to the windows.

Shit. A quick check of the time and I realise I've only got a few minutes left, best do it now or I *will* forget. Neil may be an arsehole, but he is right about one thing: if I don't pull those curtains across, and PC Cummingsly does walk by, I'll be one step closer to kipping on the Z-bed at Mum's house.

That doesn't even bear thinking about. Fuck, I can hear the *sigh* from here.

I open the flap separating the punters from the employees and make my way to the front door. Gotta make sure that's locked up first, or you end up with a straggler wandering in from a stag do, pocket full of change and a bladder full of piss. At this time of night they think they're either invincible, a comedian, or worst of all, both – and none of those options are accurate or welcome. I slide the bolt across and pull the smallest curtain in the entire world to cover the equally tiny frosted-glass window. More crap John found from somewhere.

I'm on autopilot as I shut the curtains by Dion and Mattie, first taking care not to knock over their empty glasses, and then picking them all up for a quick stop off at the bar. Paul tries distracting me with a barrage of questions about where John is, what he's doing, what he could be watching, and whether I prefer Blur or Oasis, so it's only when I get to the last set of windows that I notice it.

The Dark Horse isn't down the busiest road, but we're not tucked away on a quiet cul-de-sac at the arse end of town either. But as I stand there with a curtain in each hand, trying to blank out Paul's incessant yapping, I see that there is nothing outside. Not as in there's no people, cars, or even lamp posts, but that there is *nothing* there. Fuck. All. Completely blank. I rest my hands on the windowsill and crane my neck up, trying to make out the sky above where the closed shops should be – across the road from us.

Nothing. No shops, no road, and no sky. Not even one solitary star is shining. For a moment, the rational part of me concludes that it's just a power cut. I try to remember where the candles are. Will the pumps still work? What about the till? This is quickly replaced by more outlandish suggestions. Are we under quarantine? Has some prankster pasted paper on the windows outside? Or has a pissed-off deity wrapped us up in ribbon, every intention of gifting us to one of their chums who could make better use of our pitiful souls – mould us all into something more, something better?

I want to prove my stupid theories wrong, so I take one of the windows off the latch and give it a shove. My brain dares me to stick a hand out first, and only when it agrees with me that it feels safe enough does it let me stick my head out. The air is cool, but I still can't see anything out there. It feels ominous; I get the feeling that someone or some*thing* is out there in the murk, watching me, watching us.

What a load of crap, I tell myself. It's just evolutionary warnings hardwired into us, none of which are applicable to the times we live in. We've stopped shitting in caves and have built nice houses to live in, sure, but it's still in our nature to distrust things, especially those that go bump in the night. I'm about to turn to Paul and interrupt his asking me if I think Tyson will win at the weekend, when I hear it.

A low, bassy thrum begins to get louder. There's still nothing out there, but I can feel the blackness shake, though whether it's the air moving or the building, I don't know. I can't even use the ground as a baseline – it's not there. Nothing is there anymore. For all the world, the pub is floating. Are we resting on something? Borne aloft? Has everything else been scrubbed from existence and we've somehow not got the memo?

I need a drink.

The sound stops growing in volume, levelling out as a constant hum. With my head still stuck outside in this barren domain, my heartbeat thudding in my neck is the only other sound. I turn back and see Paul still talking to me through the glass, but I can't hear him. I try telling him to shut the fuck up, but my words have no weight out here and die in the back of my throat.

I clamp my hands to the side of my head, but still the constant drone permeates through them and into my ears. I can feel motion. Not from anything moving out there, but from this place. We've been knocked from our lofty pedestal and we're falling, tumbling end-over-end through the void. The atmosphere out here is spongy. The air thicker. Padded. Are we a delicate ornament, swaddled in packaging so we can be safely transported somewhere? If so, where are we going? Let alone the obvious question of where the hell are we now?

There's a WUMPH and we start to slow down, an invisible parachute deployed to slow our descent. We're gliding. The droning elongates, before it starts to splinter; each component of the dirge is shattering into its constituent parts. As I try to focus on them, pick apart the layers, there's an urge building within me, telling me to abandon the sanctuary of the pub. Self-preservation kicks in and I grab hold of the window, trying to anchor myself in place. As I do, the sensation ends, replaced by the opposite, a force pushing me back inside.

The noise now has become a jumble, a cacophony of random sounds, but the overall power of it has weakened. The pressure building in my head begins to ease. Grabbing hold of the window, I'm about to yank it closed when I listen, actually fucking listen to the new sounds. They're voices. Man, woman, and child.

Some are excited, others bored, they talk over each other, at times in stereo. All of them are shuffled in with animal noises, crazed, eager, hungry. They twist and coil together, becoming snarls, empty laughs, and haunting cries. But among this jumble of nonsense, I begin to pick out individual words. It's then I realise that they all share a similarity. They are all saying the same thing over and over and over again.

"You belong to us."

Four

It's easy to understand why people demonise the night. From an early age, we're conditioned to distrust it. Told to stop playing and to get home before it settles in, that you can't do anything of merit in it, and worst of all that terrible things happen only when the sun has gone down. I can't say I subscribe to that school of thought, at least not since I started this job. I'm still at work when most people are asleep, and I can safely say that as many bad things happen during the day as they do at night.

After spending the last year or so of living in the twilight, I've found that things are presented at their clearest and most simple. It strips and peels layers of the world away, removing nuance and hue, leaving you with a more accurate black-and-white picture. If anything, doesn't it make more sense to be scared when the sun is up? The scariest things in the world happen during the day, when you're supposed to feel safe, when you've been lulled into a false sense of security. Don't you ever wonder why tragedies feel so much worse when they happen on a bright summer's day?

Right now, though, I'd kill for the sun to be up, a streetlight to shine, or a car to pass by – something to convince me that what I *think* is outside is complete bullshit. That it's just a recording, a radio show, or the consequences of a tired brain trying to coax me into telling John to shove this job up his arse and find something *normal*. A nine-to-five. Fax machines and photocopiers, drinks after work on a Friday. Nicking stationery and having your full name printed in Times New Roman on a piece of folded paper that sits on your desk. Money paid into a bank account, not folded up and slipped into a grubby brown envelope. All of that would please Mother Dearest, show her I'm making something of myself, not wasting my life pulling pints in a crappy pub.

But why should I be trying to please her – or anybody, for that matter? I've always refused to aim high, because what's the point? I'm not going to be an astronaut or an engineer. I'm not going to cure cancer or bring world peace. Think about it: how many people – in a world of billions – will ever be in a position to even come close to achieving those things? I'm not saying my life choices are set low on purpose, or I'm doing it to spite myself. It's more that I've accepted that I'm not here for that. When I left college with grades that combined to spell *one* in French, I realised that life for me is about getting from point A to point B without hurting people – or myself – in the process.

Even that simple aim seems impossible at times. So why bother at all?

If I'm being truly honest with myself, I should've strived for more, pushed myself, but it just isn't me. I've settled for middle-of-the-road out of necessity, not want. So why me, and why now? Are those voices outside here to set me on the right path, or are they here to punish me for not having tried hard enough? Or have I gone so far up my own arse that I'm arrogant enough to think it's all about me? Why can't this be about Dion, or Neil?

"What's so interesting out there?" asks Paul.

"Nothing."

I pull the curtains shut, though I swear I can still hear the broken voices outside repeating their cracked verse. Maybe I *should* tell him? He can either confirm what I thought I heard, or call me an idiot. Undoubtedly via a million more questions. Problem is, how the hell do I broach the subject? I suppose I'll just calmly tell him that there's nothing out there anymore except creepy voices that seem hellbent on owning or scaring the people inside this boozer. Even if it were *normal* people out there baying for our blood, it's not something you can just drop into conversation, is it? Plus, what part of what's happening could possibly be defined as normal right now? What the hell am I going to do?

Who are these people outside? Do they have actual bodies, or are they just disembodied voices? Are they lost? Am *I* lost? What do they look like? I heard something recently that I can't stop thinking about: when you dream, the brain is incapable of creating new faces for the cast of characters that your subconscious uses to play out whatever takes its fancy. Every person you see, every single face, belongs to someone you know, or someone you've exchanged pleasantries with, given change to, gazed at across platforms, or passed on nameless streets. Makes sense, I guess. Can you imagine what fucked-up faces your brain could come up with otherwise? Mashing noses, eyes, lips, and ears together on heads formed from the pieces of a 3-D Ed Gein jigsaw puzzle.

Though it also begs another question, one far more troubling, especially as I play back the words that countless mouths uttered at me outside. The monsters that plague those same dreams and nightmares, where do *their* faces come from? Are they stolen from creatures that lurk at the edge of our own vision? Perhaps that's why we fear the night after all. Or is it simply just a case of having watched one too many late-night movies? Is that what makes the monsters?

This is another fault of mine, making mountains out of molehills. My brain sees all these gaps and fills it with the most far-fetched things imaginable. I need a distraction, some music to try and take my mind off things. I ignore Paul's latest line of questioning and get back behind the bar, close the flap, and turn on the radio, which is piped to the clientele through a crappy set of speakers. They hang from the walls by bent nails and lengths of string. One fell off a few months back, and nearly brained this old-timer who was having his morning cup of coffee. Poor sod had his hearing aid turned off. Never even knew how close he came to having his skull caved in on his weekly excursion from the retirement home.

True to form, just like the piece of shit minibus, the stereo in the pub is equally buggered. It's been stuck on one radio station since I've been working here – an eighties station of all things, playing my pre-teen soundtrack. Days of stupid tight jeans and endless shades of brown and beige. Least it gives me the chance to zone out for a minute, try and reset. The last few bars of an Elton John number fade out, replaced by a Phil Collins one that I know it shares lyrics with, but I can't remember either. What was that song called? Wasn't the Marilyn Monroe one, something about—

"Hey, do you have a minute?" I turn to see Simon at the end of the bar.

A welcome interlude. "Sure, you want another?" By the time I've walked over I can see that he's still got a near-full glass.

"No, just wanted to ask you something, if you don't mind?"

I take a quick look round to make sure no-one else needs me. Dion and Mattie are playing one of the dog-eared board games that have been left to fester on the windowsill – another of John's bright ideas to lure families in. Of all the demographics, they're the least likely to venture inside this place. Paul is staring into space, his glass a surrogate child clutched to his chest. Charlie is still lost to the machine and Neil is whispering to Jen, looming over her as she nurses her drink. "Go on, what's up?" I ask.

He pulls out a comb, dragging it through his greasy, slicked-back hair. "What do you think it is?"

An odd one. "A comb?"

Simon laughs and continues to smooth his locks back. "Nice one. No, I meant outside."

My heart skips once before resuming again at an increased level. I feel sick. My stomach acid bubbles, the body preparing for fight or flight. I've done fuck-all except run away my entire life, why the hell would I change now? "What do you mean?"

Simon smiles. He knows, he fucking knows. Not just that, but he can probably smell the stink of fear wafting off me. He slips the comb back into his inner jacket pocket. "You know exactly what I'm talking about."

"I don't—"

"I know, how could you? How could anyone? Not something we're built to process, at least not at the beginning. But can I tell you something? Something you probably won't believe."

"Go on."

He raps the bar with his knuckles. "This, all of it, it's real enough, and the only person who can stop what's about to happen, is you. I want you to remember that… no… I *need* you to remember that. When it begins, and especially later on, when you're in so deep that you can't remember a time this didn't exist, when you're wondering how the hell it got so bad, I want you to remember that you could have stopped it before it even began. But you won't. No one ever does in the beginning. We'll see later on if you're one of the people who changes their minds. For what it's worth, my money's on you to do the right thing."

"What's about to happen? Are you on about those voices outside?"

Simon nods.

"What I heard out there can't be real, we'd know about it otherwise. We'd have stories in the papers and on the news, not some weirdo in a pub trying to scare the employees."

Simon chuckles, retrieving another cigarette before closing the packet up and tapping the end on the box. "I get it, you don't know me from Adam, and here we are talking about things you couldn't even imagine existing until a few minutes ago. Things that everyone subconsciously spends their entire lives running away from. Sooner or later, they catch up with you. No-one is exempt, not even me. But I assure you that everything I've said is true… and more. How about I make you a deal? I can do one thing right now which will prove that this is very, very real. From there on in, armed with that bit of knowledge, you can do as you see fit."

"Prove what? I don't understand."

"You will do," Simon stands up and straightens out his trenchcoat.

I rest my hands on the edge of the bar and fix him a stare, trying to look as believable as possible. "Whatever you're going to do, whatever you think is outside, you're wrong. Monsters, proper ones, with big fuck-off teeth and glow-in-the-dark eyes, they don't exist."

"Oh, I know. There are far worse things than monsters. Trust me." Breaking my glare, Simon looks over my shoulder towards the front door. He calls out across the space between him and the person sitting there. "Paul, it's time to go now." He puts the cigarette in his mouth and cups it with his free hand before using his own lighter to get it to life. As the end starts to smoulder, he points it at the door, the barrel of a smoking gun. "Cheerio."

Without question or debate, Paul stands up, puts his glass down and heads for the door. His hand is on the bolt before I've even said a word. By the time I do, he's slid it free. "No! Wait!" I scream.

Everyone stops what they're doing and turns to stare at me.

Through the crappy speakers the bloke from Genesis and the tune whose name I still can't remember fades away to be replaced by Tina Turner. Paul – still facing the door – says over his shoulder, "It's okay. I've got to go now. It's my time."

"No you don't. What are you listening to this bloke for? Do you know him or something?"

Paul shrugs, still fiddling with the door mechanism; I can hear the hinges sigh as they begin their outward motion. "No. But if he says it's time to go, who am I to argue?"

I'm standing behind him now. "Mate, it's what you do. You're always asking people what they're doing and why – it's pretty annoying, if I'm being honest with you. So I'm finding it a little hard to believe that you're going to let a complete stranger tell you what to do."

He looks past me at Simon, who raises his pint in silent salute. "I dunno, he's right, though. It is time to go, night." With that, he opens the door and steps outside, the door closing softly behind him. My hand shoots out and grabs the handle; a voice inside me demands that I wrench it open, tell him he's a stupid sod and to get back inside, tell him I'll take his place. That sounds noble and the right thing to do. But… there's another nagging voice: quieter, yet firmer. What if I wasn't hearing things? What if it *is* real?

"Go on. What's stopping you?" Simon asks, his voice travelling across the expanse. "What's so scary about going out there?" Everyone is looking at me now, frozen in time. The only one in motion is Simon, who places his drink on the bar and flicks the ash from his cigarette.

I want it to stop. That old feeling of helplessness closes around my heart once more. I'm smothered in the duvet of my childhood bed, trying to squeeze myself so tight that I might disappear into nothing if I do it properly. Listening out for the shouting downstairs, the aftermath of my latest misstep, sometimes by intention, often by accident. Sausages put in the freezer. Handwritten notes stuck to the fridge door with curling Sellotape. THIS ONE, YOU FUCKING IDIOT. Lesson delivered and underlined in felt pen. Close myself off again. Don't let anything in. Don't let anything out. No escape. No surrender. Dig in for the long haul, no matter how far they push you. Things won't be this way forever. But inaction can *feel* like forever.

My fingers are still frozen around the door handle. Deep down inside me, it stirs, that lost little child, head protruding from the bedding, telling me that I know what I should do. Open the door, swap places. Him for me. It would be so easy to do, and the right thing. But I can't. I'm scared. Scared of so many things. But right here and now, the pub being set adrift in nothingness, the feeling of being pushed and pulled, those voices that still echo in my head, all are stopping me from doing what I know I should. Paul, the poor bastard, doesn't have the slightest clue what's out there.

But I do.

Don't I?

"He's had a good innings, though gone too young, wouldn't you say?" Simon offers. I trudge over to Paul's vacant table and pull the curtains open.

There's still nothing out there. Through the window. by the hint of illumination from within this haven, I can just make out Paul's silhouette. He's floating, waiting, as if a taxi is going to roll along at any minute and pick him up. The voices chatter faster, mingling with their animal counterparts, until they all lose distinction and meld as one, becoming a singular, bassy note of doom. The sound buffets the building, shaking us as we hang in the nothingness, the panes rattling in their frames. Then, the tsunami of sound stops. In the lull, Paul disappears. One minute he's there, the next, nothing. Just the eternal blackness of the surrounding night. Sound rumbles from afar; as the wave hits us, so does Paul. His face slams against the bottom half of the window, causing it to crack. His head is misshapen, the skull shattered, pieces of bone rattle together beneath the sagging skin. The force has blown one of his eyeballs from its socket and it hangs from the bloodied sodden grotto. The downward motion of the building begins again as the sound returns to its original level. As Paul is slowly dragged upwards, the eyeball glares at me, leaving a trail of slime behind it as it glides up the glass.

A bone has burst through the palm of his hand, and it screeches and scratches against the glass as he rises. His fat swollen tongue lolls between cracked teeth; the tip slobbers and licks the window on the journey upwards. His body has been compacted into a dwarven version of himself, his torso concertinaed into a bodice, arms jutting out sideways as if they've had too much pressure applied internally. As he is reeled in from the heavens, his body begins to separate out, his broken spine a grotesque parody of a serpent as it slinks and slithers sideways up the glass.

Finally, Paul comes to a rest, his crushed, deformed body framed by the window. His errant eye looks at me, the pupil dilates, then the building shakes, ridding itself of its unwanted parasite and he is cast free.

Past the etched glass, I see him float away until he is gone, devoured by the hungry night, and all I'm left with are charcoal rubbings of aftersight.

Throughout it all, the woman from the Thunderdome has been asking what love has got to do with fucking *anything*.

Five

What do I do? Perhaps someone here will have a clue? Turning around in my search for life, I see that everyone is already back to what they were doing before, as if nothing has happened. Charlie digs me in the ribs, shaking his glass. "Best get ready to rustle me up another."

I mumble my reply. "Sure, no problem."

He slaps the side of the machine as another stake gets swallowed up inside. "Good on ya, see if you can pour me some luck whilst you're at it, too. I'm on a proper losing streak tonight."

Aren't we all?

I lift the wooden flap and let it clatter behind me, making Neil jump. "Watch it," he warns, but his threats are as hollow as this place feels right now. There's an excited shout from the corner; I look across, hoping that either Dion or Mattie have seen something too, but it's just a beneficial dice roll that was deemed worthy of their celebration. The murmur of the pub blends into one: voices indistinct, faces a blur. The inside morphs into the antithesis of the world beyond these four walls, we are the light to the dark that lurks beyond this chamber of stone.

From the corner of the bar I hear a click of fingers, and the world locks back into focus again. With a crooked finger, Simon beckons me over. "Well? Have I turned you into a believer?"

"What is it? What's out there?"

"You can't do anything about Paul now, but you can about the others."

"Drop the riddles and just fucking tell me!"

Simon waves his hand around the bar, capturing everyone with an invisible lasso. "The people in this place are here because of *you*."

I only realise my fists are clenched when I feel my nails digging into the palms of my hands. Then my body rings out with the warning signs. Eyes: wider. Nostrils: flared. Teeth: gritted. My chest does not move in time with my breathing, it's a breastplate of flesh-and-bone, the outer layer of my bullshit armour. I can feel my muscles tense. It's the mirror of the actions I don't want to repeat. Of what I've always said I don't want to become.

But it's there.

Right. Fucking. There.

Her words are my thoughts now. *You can't let him get away with that. Do something, you useless sack of shit. Are you just going to stand there and do nothing?*

And the worst: *I'm disappointed in you.*

They're the four words that send a signal to the lifeguard, telling them the tide is about to break.

Simon swirls his glass. "You know it doesn't matter, don't you?"

"What?"

He pokes me in the top of my chest. "All of that *stuff*, it's irrelevant. Why are you holding onto it? What purpose does it serve? Where has it ever got you?"

"I don't—"

"Understand. I know. It's a pity, really, it is. I wish there were some other way we could do this, you and

I, but we only have a finite amount of time together. How you spend it is down to you, and the endgame is unfortunately the same."

"Then why do it? Why is this happening to me?"

Simon leans across the bar. "I've said already. It happens to everyone – to you, Neil, Jennifer, Dion, Matilda, Charles. Even Paul. Everyone has a reckoning which is theirs alone to face, but for some, it offers something different."

"What? What does it offer?"

"Hope. Redemption," he says, and sits back on his bar stool. "Peace."

My head is spinning. I feel I'm on the cusp of some higher understanding. Those nights walking home when you look up at the sky, and for one transient moment you think you get it. Not everything, that's impossible. But you feel something. A connection. From this compacted crush of atoms to another, maybe not even in a form you're aware of. It's fleeting, and the more you try to grab it, the more it evaporates, leaving you with nothing but air. But you *have* experienced it. You know it's real. You feel like you don't need to push so hard to find answers to those deep and meaningful questions, because you've caught a glimpse of something more.

Simon rolls up his sleeve and taps his wristwatch. "Anyway, we've got to get a move on. Things to do, places to go, et cetera."

"Are you off?"

He laughs. A genuine laugh, too. "Not me." He puts his fingers in his mouth and wolf-whistles. "Charlie. Time to go, me ol' mucker."

Charlie is just about to feed more money into the belly of the fruit machine when he hears Simon call his name. The coins slip from his fingers into the slot as the words hit him and he goes perfectly still. Ignoring the allure of the lights and the bells and the whistles, urging him to nudge, hold, double his bet for better odds, he turns on his heels and heads for the door.

I plead. "Not him, come on, what's he ever done?"

"Everything and nothing, and a little in between. It doesn't matter what, there's only one way of stopping him going out through that front door." He taps his wristwatch again. "Tick-tock."

I can't even bear to try and stop him leaving. The scratch on the window from Paul's departure is a reminder of my last failure; what can I do? What have I ever been able to do? I can't stop the weeds sprouting between the cracks, I can't change people's minds. I'm just me. Winging life one day at a time.

I'm the centre of everyone's attention again, as if I'm the keynote speaker at a conference and they're expecting a rousing speech. Problem is, I've lost my notes and have to resort to what I've always done. Adapt. Survive. Even now, my biggest concern is that they won't laugh at my shitty jokes. Charlie opens the door, looks over at me, and smiles that crooked smile. "Looks like my luck is changing at last, huh?"

"Cheerio, chum," Simon calls out, and the bar is one person less.

Even after he closes the door, everyone is still staring at me. "What?" Nothing. No response. "What do you want me to do?" Part of me wants to see what's happening out there. I've not heard anything since he left, perhaps he'll be spared? Perhaps Charlie is one of the good ones, and whatever it is that's out there will see he's not a threat, and that—

The sound of glass breaking happens just before Charlie's body slams into the fruity he's been trying – and failing – to bleed dry all night. The impact causes the machine to tip backwards, before it settles on its base. His sudden reappearance in the bar makes those who remain return to their activities – like one of their friends hasn't just been hurled through the window of their local. It can't be real. This has got to be a prank. A dummy or something, all part of some plot to try and tip me over the edge. All shits and giggles. An initiation into the wacky world of The Dark Horse after hours.

But it sure as shit looks real to me. Shards of glass disintegrate even further as I crush them underfoot. A finger, with a golden sovereign ring still attached, rolls across the carpet. Charlie is well and truly embedded into the body of the machine. I consider how lucky I am to be spared the sight of his ruined face, no doubt sliced to ribbons after having been launched through one window and then into the glass and metal of the gambling façade. His legs are grazing the floor behind him. It reminds me of the time a few months back when he got so pissed that Dion and I had to carry him home. I say *carry*, it was more like *dragging* him home. The one abiding memory of that trip was the sound of leather being scuffed against the pavement, his shoes being slowly scoured away. I remember worrying that we'd end up sanding his toes down to nubs of bone.

Limp arms hang either side of the main console. The hand with the missing finger is twitching. His brain is still telling him to play the game, win his stake back. Thick gloopy blood rappels down from the stump of his index finger. It reaches for the carpet before spooling back up. Coalescing into a thick droplet, it finally falls free and hits the carpet. The blood resists at first, before soaking into the weave. Glass and parts of the window frame form irregular-shaped spines which stick out of his body.

"Oi." Neil's voice forces me to drag my attention away from Charlie's body. The fat fuck taps his empty glass with his dumpy fingers. "When you've quite finished gawping, I'll have another."

"When I've quite finished?" I point back at the corpse. "I think this is a bit more fucking pressing, don't you?"

"It was his time to go, and now he's gone. So why don't you drop the attitude and fix me up a refill?"

I can hear cogs and pulleys working away in the broken machine. Snagging and pulling on decrepit and rent-open skin. Within me, something clicks. *My* machine is breaking, too. "Charlie is dead, and all you can think about is getting another drink?"

"Well he ain't gonna need one, is he?"

"He has a point, you know," Dion concurs.

"I'm sorry. You all seem remarkably calm considering Charlie has just been thrown through the fucking window."

Neil shrugs. "He finally managed to hit double-top at long bloody last."

"Oh, bravo," adds Dion.

"Could've done with that earlier against the Royal Oak. Might've wrapped things up a bit quicker, got home before… you know," Mattie joins in.

"What is wrong with you lot? I'm going to call someone," I say, and set off to the phone behind the bar. I need to do something, and right now, practical things are pretty much the only thing on my mind.

"Who are you going to call?" Dion asks.

"Ghostbusters!" Neil shouts, and everyone laughs and cheers.

Fucking pissheads. Let's dial 999, get the ambulance here – the police, too? I dunno, who calls the people to come out with the black van so they can take away the body? Don't think the paramedics will do that. "I wouldn't bother if I were you," says Simon, as I slam the telephone on the bar top.

I ignore him – he's got to be the one behind all this, I don't know how, but he has to be. Though none of the others seem to know he's even here. I dial the three numbers before putting the handset to my ear.

Nothing. No dial tone. No voice from the other end reeling off choices. Absolutely sod-all.

I tap the button where the handset normally lies, trying to carry out phone-CPR. But like Charlie and Paul, it's dead. "I told you so," mutters Simon.

Got to be a setup. I pick up the wire and trace it with my fingers to the socket on the wall. It's in; no nicks or cuts in the wire as far as I can see. I take the plug out, blow on the end as if I know what the fuck I'm doing, and then shove it back into the hole with a satisfying click. I pick up the handset again and get the same result. Dead air. Not even dialling zero – which should reach John upstairs – makes anything happen.

"That's pointless even trying, too," Simon drawls.

Hang on – even if I can't phone him upstairs, I can still go and see him. Lazy bastard is probably up watching some shitty film, or trying to work out the rules to baseball. I shove the phone back on its shelf and head back down the bar. "Are you going to serve me at some point?" Neil asks. I ignore him.

The door to the upstairs flat is opposite my little perch by the stereo; Tears For Fears are lamenting the lunacy of the world as I grab hold of the handle and twist. The door opens with no trouble at all, except that on the other side – where the stairs should be – there is nothing but wall.

"I told you," says Simon.

I can't quite believe what I'm seeing. The door is nothing but an aesthetic home accessory serving as much use as a vase. But at least you can put something in that; this door is just a piece of wood opening up to nothing and nowhere. I knock on the wall and get nothing back except a dull thud telling me that it's solid enough. Even so, I bang on it a few more times, achieving nothing but numbing my hand. I slam the door shut and turn back to the man at the end of the bar. "Alright, what the fuck is going on here? Where am I?"

Simon starts clapping. "Bingo!"

Marching across to him, I can feel the red mist descending once more. "What the fuck have you done?"

"Me? Nothing at all. As I said, this is all on you. I'm just glad that you're finally starting to ask the right questions. I was wondering if you ever would."

"Are you going to start making sense at some point?" We're now face-to-face.

Simon pushes his empty glass to me. "First, let me get a round in." Everyone hoots and hollers. "Then someone – and by that I mean *you* – has a choice to make."

Six

Everyone's starting to get lairy now. The drunken bravado that turns regular people into complete dickheads is spreading throughout the survivors. Dion and Mattie have ditched their table and are perched on bar stools. The whole gang's here, and chief amongst them all is the guy who – up until this evening – no-one had ever met before.

As I'm pouring Neil's pint, Dion crunches up his bag of Scampi Fries. Resting small pieces on the palm of one hand, he flicks them at me, scoring arbitrary points as they bounce off different parts of my face. Mattie is howling with laughter, telling him, "get his nose". BONK. Ten points. "Hit his ear!" I duck, and the chunk of stinky snack disappears behind the phone book at the end of the bar. She boos at his effort and mine. It's little respite. "Hit 'im on the forehead!" BONK. Twenty points.

I want to punch him. At the very least smack his hand and make him drop his ammunition. A one-eyed swaying shot aimed into my mouth cannons off my cheek and lands in the last vestiges of Neil's pint. This makes Dion and Mattie go, "oooohhhh," and hide behind their hands, expecting a response but knowing that for all of his faults – and he has many – the last thing Neil is going to do is swing for either of them.

The ricochet has at least brought about an end to the irritation. The pair of them elbow each other, before Dion asks for two glasses of red. I pour them and turn to Simon. "Another pint of Guinness, if you please." I clear some of the empties and begin to pour his drink. "It's nice to see everyone in one place. Makes it easier."

"For what?"

"Makes it more of a community – you can't beat these places, bringing people together. Just think, without this pub, you might never have met. What would your lives have been like if you hadn't?"

"It's a small town, pretty sure people would've met in other ways," I reply, trying to focus on getting his beverage to the mark where I can let it rest. It's got to be spot-on, perfect. Devil is in the details. I don't mind being spontaneous; many a good – and stupid – thing has happened from just saying *fuck it* and going with the flow, but if you do something, may as well do it properly. A reason for everything. Don't waste energy on something if it doesn't need doing now. That's me.

People say that in itself is a contradiction. But then, in many ways, so am I. Hate the heat, but love the cold. Yet as soon as you tell someone you're going on a beach holiday, they say "Ah-ha!" as if they've caught you out in a trap of your own making. Who am I trying to please, them or me? They say it's impossible to be spontaneous if you plan. How does that work? Who the fuck is out there making the rules of what you can and can't do with your life? I'm not hurting anyone.

I can be strong, but other times I cry at the slightest thing, and I'm talking real stupid stuff. A character dying on a soap opera, or one of those feel-good segments they tag on to the end of the news to try and take your mind off the fucking awfulness of the world.

Cry. Keep it in. Show weakness. Don't you fucking dare. Fight. Take it. Run. Walk. Crawl on your fucking belly until your pathetic skin tears open. Watch on as your insides spill out and you lie stranded in your own disgusting mess. Further confirmation, if it were even needed, that the whole goddamn world doesn't have a clue what to do, so it just shouts at you until you do something that fits the current mood. Why do we have to contort ourselves into shapes so we can be told that we fit in? That *now* we belong. Until the next fad rolls around and we're rendered obsolete once more.

That's why we should just live for the moment. That one sweet fucking moment. And not just because of the trite bullshit that it could be our last. Yes, it could be, but you know what is more likely? That it's just the latest in a string of moments that reaches out back across time to where we were pushed out screaming into this world, and even before that moment of suffering. It'll drag out until the moment we curl up and die. And like the beginning, it'll reach out beyond that, too. We spend our lives being so fucking scared of acting how other people expect us to that we forget the most important thing. The only person you will ever understand, ever empathise totally with… is you. So quit trying to be someone – or something – you ain't.

"And are you scared?" Simon asks.

"Of what?"

"Of now, of then, of what's to come."

I top up his drink and place it in front of him. "I've spent my entire life being afraid of one thing or another."

"And where has it got you?"

I tap the thick wooden bar. "Here. Now."

"Is it where you want to be?"

"No. But there's time."

He laughs. "If I had a penny for every time I've heard that…"

I rest my forearms on the bar. "What *is* this? Who are you? Really?"

"A better question would be *when*."

"Fine, *when* is this?"

He smiles. "Now."

"Aren't you the comedian. Fifteen-eighty, please."

He fishes inside his pocket and passes me a twenty. "Get one for yourself."

"I think that's the most sensible thing you've said all night, don't mind if I do" I scan the optics before settling on a double Southern Comfort.

"With everything you've been through tonight, and what's about to happen next, you've earned it."

"And what is about to happen next?"

"I've told you already. A choice."

"Between what?" I neck the drink and get another double; the warm fuzzy feeling runs down my body, trying to wash the guilt away.

He takes the change from me and pockets it. "Not between what," he says, nodding at the quartet lined up at the bar, "but between *whom*."

As I slam the till shut, Simon raps his lighter on the end of Jen's empty tonic bottle. "Ladies and gentlemen, if I may have your attention." Silence reigns. "Thank you. We're gathered here today because of one person, and it's now time for them to make a simple choice." Dion drums on the bar and Mattie tries to make a trumpet sound to join in as herald. "As you all know, Paul and Charles have had their time and they've had to go. A terrible shame and we shall miss them terribly. But alas… it is now time for one more of you to exit stage left."

Dion begins to boo theatrically, Mattie joins in, throwing errant filter tips at Simon, who seems to revel in the role of jester. Simon talks over the building ruckus. "Fear not, for the next person to depart will be decided by our barkeep. If you please."

None of them look perturbed in the slightest. They may have missed seeing Paul's broken body get thrown against the window, but every single one of them saw Charlie's head-first entrance back into the bar. Even if they didn't, they sure as hell can't miss the body that's still wedged in the fruit machine.

"No. I won't," I say, trying to sound stronger than I feel.

Dion begins to boo again, cupping his hands around his mouth. Mattie swings on her stool, trying to jab me. "Play the game, you idiot. Come on, choose! What're you scared of?"

Neil joins in, baiting me. "Come on, are you chicken or something? Just say a name. That's all."

The only one who is quiet is Jen, lost in her own world, where she seems to spend most of her time.

Simon shoves a hand in his jacket pocket. "Won't, or can't?"

"What's the difference?"

"A whole world apart. Come on now, choose."

"Fine," I say, shutting them up. Dion cheers as he and Mattie sidle up to each other. I point at Simon. "You. I choose you. Off you pop."

Dion begins to drum the bar again. "Oooohhhh, cheeky."

Simon laughs. "I'm afraid I'm the only one who's off the table. Call it a perk of the job."

"What job?"

"I told you. Debt collector. Now choose."

"I can't, how can I? Why do I have to?"

"See, it's gone from *won't* to *can't*. Which one is the truth, I wonder?"

"It's impossible, you're asking me to pick someone to go out *there*."

Simon leans on the bar, angled out to face the crowd. "And what is out there?"

"I don't know what's out there, or even what's in here. All I know is that whoever I choose won't be coming back, and that is something that I can't live with."

"You're getting ahead of yourself." Simon draws a four-leaf clover in the foam of his Guinness. "Do you want to know why you are the one who gets to make the choice?" I nod. "The only reason these people are in this mess in the first place is because of you. Conveniently, you're also the only person that can get them out of it, one way or another. Now, I really must insist. Choose, or I'll send every single one of them out there."

From where I'm stood, backed into the corner of the bar by the potted plants, Simon and I are so close together that I can see the lines around his eyes. The notches in his skin. Old acne pockmarks. One of his eyes is more open than the other, the latter looking bored with it all as its sibling stares in eager anticipation. His hair is starched with smoke and grease. He has an unwashed smell about him, but it's not overpowering.

"What did I do that means it's all on me?"

"We'll get to that, in time. Pick one."

"I don't know how."

"What do you mean, you don't know how? You woke up and chose what to wear, didn't you? You opened the cupboard and selected what to have for breakfast. Your appearance at work today was another choice, one you made without forethought or ponderance, so why the hesitation now?"

I point to Charlie's corpse. "Because none of those choices led to something like that."

Simon grins: this thing is an evil one. His eye teeth pop over his bottom lip and hook into them, anchoring it in place. "You'd be surprised what your choices have led to through the course of your life." He lets the words hang there, the musty stench of his body filling the space between us. "Now. Choose."

I gulp. "No."

"What if the choice was just between Neil and Jennifer? Does that make it easier at all? One from two?" I shake my head.

"Spineless," grumbles Neil.

Simon looks past me at Dion. "Be a good fellow and get those playing cards, will you?" I hear feet trudging off behind me before the pack of cards hits the bar. "Fine. Then perhaps we'll just leave it to luck. Fate. Or maybe even God."

"There's no such thing."

"As what? Luck, fate or God?"

"Not sure about any of them, but I'm pretty sure there's no god, not with everything that goes on in the world." One of my earliest certainties, so proud. Unshakeable. Yet it's bothered me that in itself, that constitutes a belief in something. Is that a paradox? Is believing in nothing the same as believing in *some*thing?

Simon smiles. "An interesting notion, but have you considered a simpler question – what is a god? Truly? Is it something which determines who lives and who dies? That sounds plausible. Whether it's money, or love, or any of the near-endless things to which you could dedicate your life in the hope of attaining its affection, isn't that a god?"

"I don't—"

Simon digs the cards from the box and holds them out to me. "Everything you cling to, your values, your beliefs, are they not your god? Right here and now, aren't they dictating your thoughts and actions? Does that mean you're your own god? Which in turn makes you your own slave. Caught forever twixt dusk and dawn. Right and wrong. Trying to live in the moment as you dare to look forward." I look at the dog-eared deck of cards in front of me. "Why not let go of that this time? If you can't truly decide then pass the beacon over to something outside of your control. Let these be your judge. They're impartial, and if the decision turns out to be one you don't like, you can just say 'it wasn't me' – how does that sound?"

From outside, I hear the thunder begin to build into a growl of a warning which shakes the building. Simon stands sentinel. "Take them." The glasses on the bar begin to shimmy and judder as the noise reverberates through the walls, overpowering the music from the tinny speakers. He lowers his voice. "Take them. Now."

"Fine." The instant I pick up the tatty cards, the sound outside stops; the radio loses its signal before the Pet Shop Boys get back to reminding everyone that it's a sin. I shuffle the deck; they've lived in the pub for the entire time I've worked here, countless fingers having leafed through them, coating them in grotty layers of grime. A few of them have been bent over at the corner, no doubt in an attempt to gain favour.

"That'll do. Now, let Neil and Jennifer pick."

"Please, look, there has to be another way. Can I—"

Simon slams his fist on the bar. "Enough! No more stalling. One of them has to go, and they have to go *now*. I've tried to show you some understanding, but no more. Perhaps you want to go in their place?"

Why don't I? It would mean that I don't have to go on with his… *whatever* it is, anymore. But it doesn't feel right yet. I've yet to arrive at a conclusion that will let me willingly open that door and step out there. But at what cost to this quartet of unfortunate association? We're not family, not even close, but does it make me a bad person for letting them take what should undoubtedly be my place?

That's what this is about, isn't it? That's what Simon is angling for. That all of this will simply go away if it were me that upped and left. What am I scared of? What is it that's keeping me here? I've nothing and no-one, and the times I wished I could just vanish without a trace are beyond counting. Well, here's my chance, right here and now. Throw these cards into the air and just fucking leave. But I can't. I feel incomplete.

"Well?" Simon asks.

I fan out the cards; some stick to each other with stale beer and bits of food. The white lacquer has turned a jaundiced yellow from the tobacco smoke that coats everything which dares to linger in this place.

"High card wins. Or loses. Depending on your point of view," he confirms.

"Why don't we get a go?" asks Dion

"It's not your time yet," Simon smirks.

"Spoilsport."

Neil takes a big swig of his beer, rifles through the cards, and picks one out. He doesn't even look at it before placing it face-up on the bar in front of him. "Jack of hearts."

I look across to Jen, who has already chosen her card. She turns it over and lays it down flat. "King of spades."

"See, that wasn't too difficult now, was it?" Simon takes the cards from me and places them on the bar.

I have to say something. "Jen, I'm sorry, I really am, if I—"

Simon butts in. "Jennifer, if you please." He points at the door, the broken glass a most unwelcome mat.

She stands up without missing a beat and heads for the exit. I call out, "wait," and she stops mid-stride.

"Yes? Is there someone else you'd prefer to go instead?" I can see Simon from the corner of my eyes.

I nod. "Yeah."

"Well?"

"It's between them?"

"Correct."

"Then I choose Neil."

"Are you sure?"

I nod again. "Yeah. I'm sure."

"Then Neil, would you mind terribly, taking your wife's place?"

Neil places his drink on the bar and passes his wife as she makes her way back. "Bye, love," she mumbles. Without missing a beat, her husband opens the door. From outside, I can hear the multitude of voices talking over each other; they all fall silent the instant the new arrival enters their domain. There's a click as the door closes, followed by a snap of bone. The doleful choir begins their monotonal chanting again. I half-expect another delivery through the window, but nothing comes. Dion has picked up the cards and is leafing through them, showing off hand-drawn cocks, or reading aloud jokes usually found as graffiti on the walls of toilet cubicles. Mattie titters as he holds court. Through it all, Jen is checking the front door, hoping that Neil is going to return, a single tear falling down her cheek.

She knows.

She knows her husband isn't coming back. And for everything he's done, for all the misery he's undoubtedly caused her, a part of her is crushed. That's something I've never had. Judging by the events of the night, I'm not sure it's something I'm ever going to have. I look around at who's left, stopping at Simon. I can see that he's thinking the same thing as me: who's next?

Seven

For the first time tonight, someone who has gone is missed. Finally, someone other than me is remotely bothered that we're one person less. I get that, I really do, but I'm still surprised to see Jen cry.

"Do you want a drink?" That gets her attention. She turns to me with inside-out eyes, more red than white. Steamed and ready to burst. She grips her glass so tightly that for a moment, I think it's going to shatter between her fingers.

"Go on, then," she says, and necks the last of her drink. "Make it a double, will you?"

As I put down her glass, it nestles on the beer towel next to the dregs of her husband's pint, his smudged lip-print on the rim, his fingerprints staining the side of the glass. I catch Jen looking at it too, threatening to set her off again.

I'm rubbish at this. People, I mean. Trying to make them feel better, helping them when they need it. No matter what I say, it never seems to be the right thing, never seems enough – like tackling a raging forest fire with a paltry glass of water. My mum often accused me of not listening. Which always struck me as an odd thing to say to someone, especially if you're accusing them of not paying attention in the first place. Wasted words. But she knew. She always knew, even if I would swear blind that I was the one in the right. Whether it was tough love or reverse psychology, she gave it all a go. Anything to set her wayward eldest back onto the path. The path I was apparently ordained to tread.

"When people are upset, they don't want you to fix them," she said. "They don't want you to tell them what they should do, they just want you to listen." It's taken me years to understand what she meant by that.

Looking at Jen right now, those words finally make some kind of sense. Part of me wants to pick up Neil's glass, pour away the dregs, shove it into the washer and scrub the last part of him from this place. But she is looking at it, studying the loops and whorls of his fingerprints as if it were his face. "Are you okay?" A stupid question. How can she be okay? But I don't know what else to say. How to start. I can't say I hold either person in high regard, but I'm not a selfish arsehole. If someone is suffering, you have to see if you can help, even if that means you have to ask the dumbest question possible to start that process off.

She chuckles, undoubtedly thinking the same thing. Shared humanity in all of *this*. She sniffs and wipes her nose on the sleeve of her jumper. "Did you know that we met in here? Neil and me." I shake my head as she points over to the fruit machine – where Charlie still twitches. "Course, they had the pool table there back then. Used to come in here during lunchtime from college. He'd be with his friends, me with mine, we knew each other, but only just to say hello. Nothing major." Jen swirls the glass, mixing the gin and tonic together. "First time we ever properly spoke was when I—" She smiles, her eyes glazing over as she recalls the moment. "I was stripes, Shelley was plain. I'd cleared up and was trying to pot the eight-ball into the far-left corner, over by that window. Don't know how I managed it, but I completely shanked the shot. The ball sailed over the cushion and just took off. You know those moments where everything slows down? Where you know what's going to happen, but you can't do anything about it? Well, Neil's chatting to his mate, Kevin Godfrey, I think his name was, and for some reason he turns his head just as the ball comes sailing through thin air. CLUNK. Smacks him right in the middle of his forehead." Jen touches the spot on her face, her fingers lingering there, tracing an indelible mark.

"The place goes quiet. By the time the cue ball has hit the floor and rolled underneath the table, there's a bump already coming up on his noggin." Jen starts to chuckle and takes a mouthful of G&T. "Everyone is on pause, it's like the only two people that can move are me and him, and all I can do is gawp. He ducks under the table and comes back up with the ball. He walks over, hands it to me, and closes my fingers round it. 'Foul shot,' he says. I see something in him then. Something beyond that wall he puts up. I ask him if he's okay and he just laughs, says he's had worse, and I don't doubt it. I don't know what to do, so I pick up my glass, neck the contents, and tip what's left of the ice cubes into my hand. Standing on tiptoes, I press it against the bump, which feels so hot that I worry it's going to melt the ice and drip water all over him. He holds his hand over mine and we just stand there. Me looking up at him, him down at me. It's one of those moments in life that you never forget. You can't."

"What happened next?"

Jen smiles. "As I went to pull my hand away, I accidentally swung the cue up and hit him in the balls. You should've heard the things he came out with. Had to put all his change in the swear jar. Do you know what he told me later?" I shake my head as she looks at me straight. "That it was worth it. That *I* was worth it."

Sentimentality is one of mankind's curses. It grants us the ability to look at the past with rose-tinted glasses. "But didn't Neil... you know?" I blurt out. In that moment, I encapsulate what our species does by default, that we always find it easier to break instead of build.

"What do you mean?"

It's a crossroads. I could acquiesce and apologise. Backtrack and cover over what I've just said. "He always seems... *seemed* overpowering. Did he hurt you?"

Or not.

"My husband was many things, but he never laid a finger on me."

"I'm sorry, just we all... I mean I—"

"I know what people think, what you all think. Neil saved me. No-one else did."

"But aren't you just protecting him?"

She slams her glass on the bar, grabs hold of her sleeve and pulls it up. Turning her arm over, I see ribbon scars running up and down from wrist to bicep. Her body trembles as she bares her scarred skin. This exhibition is borne from anger, not the kind you use for power or dominance, but the kind you reserve for when you are forced to reveal something you don't want to. That you shouldn't have to.

Some things you have to keep inside. They're too terrible to share with people, especially people like me. What business is it of mine? "Look. Go on. Take a good look. Take a good look at what Jennifer did to herself. Is that what you want? Hmm? Make you feel better for knowing?"

"No. I'm sorry, really I am, it's not—" What can I say? It would be as if I had lain all my burdens upon her. Those dirty secrets, those lies. The things you keep hidden because you know that people will look at you differently afterwards – for better or for worse.

"Neil saved me. From this. From more than you'll ever know."

"But what about the way he treats people – what about them? What about you?"

"I never said he was a saint."

How do you put the genie back in the bottle – use up all your wishes? And what on? Frivolous things so you can expend your good fortune and return to square one? Or do you decide that this time, you're going to do things differently? You're not going to hide behind excuses anymore. You won't resort to walking away. You're going to stand tall and face what you've done, and no matter what happens, you're going to sort out this fucking mess you made. "Tell me about him."

The question throws her. "What do you mean?"

"I guess I got it wrong about Neil. I thought I knew what kind of person he was, but all I really knew was what I *thought* he was, not what he actually was. So tell me about him. What made you fall in love with him?"

"He didn't try to fix me. He let me be me. But all the things I did, the times when everything got too much, and I'd root around for a blade, or a shard of glass, hack at myself to take the pain away – he became the only person who could help me. Not overnight, but gradually. He showed me I could trust him. That I didn't have to drink myself into oblivion every night.

It made me see another way. He helped me to control it. He gave me an option, another way. And for that, I will always love him."

"I never knew."

Jen smiles. "Why would you? How well do we really know anyone? What's on the outside isn't always what lies within. Neil would never say I couldn't drink, but he tried to let me know when I was in danger of going down the same old road. He was the only one who stood by me in those dark times, no-one else. He didn't judge me. He just listened. And when I went to him with blood trickling down my arm, he didn't tell me off, he held me. Told me it would be okay, and in time, it was."

"Until today."

Jen pulls down her sleeve and rests a hand on mine. "I'll always have him, no matter what."

I look at Jen and see her in a way I never have before. Yes, she's small, but that's not weakness. The quiet she cloaks herself in isn't something she's forced to wear, but part of her. She's kept all this pain and hurt in for so long, it amazes me she can even breathe.

"Do you regret your choice?" asks Simon.

"No. But I do have a question."

"Go on."

"None of this is real, is it?"

"Define reality."

I smack the bar with the palm of my hand. "Enough with the philosophy 101, why can't you just tell me?"

"Because it doesn't work that way. You can barely comprehend what you've seen already, how do I, or you, know you can handle what is really going on?"

"What's the worst that can happen?"

Simon smiles again – the one where he knows the punchline before he's even heard the first line of the joke. "True. Some might say that the worst has already happened, but I can assure you that they'd be wrong. From an outsider's point of view, things can always get a *lot* worse."

"I want to know."

"Once you do, it can't be taken back. You'll be past the point of no return, there will be nowhere you can hide."

"From what?"

Simon points to the broken window. "From *it*. After I've shown you, if you do not choose when I tell you to, or follow my instructions to the letter, there will be repercussions. Severe ones."

"I need to know. Tell me."

Simon rolls his lighter between his fingers. "I can't tell you what's happening, no-one can. The only way is to be shown. Are you sure you want to see?"

I nod once, standing up straight.

"Very well." There's a rasp of metal from the flint, and a solitary spark which blanches the world, before I'm pitched into blackness.

Eight

I don't feel right.

Something is holding me in place. It's wrapped tightly over my right shoulder, diagonally across my chest, and biting into my waist. My forehead is warm and pulsing in time with the heartbeat thumping in my neck. I'm a faulty furnace set to blow. A valve somewhere has become stuck, and if it doesn't vent soon, then it'll blow a hole through the top of my skull. I want to squeeze my nose and blow, to make my ears pop and restore some equilibrium. Some balance. It's then that I realise that I'm upside-down.

A weird discovery when you can't see anything. Granted, I can feel the pinch of this band holding me in place, but there is no horizon for me to adjust to, so I must be floating. My eyes are tight shut – chances are they've glimpsed what's out there, and are trying to protect me from an unknown horror that will devour me if I dare look upon it.

The fear is all-consuming. Where am I? Is it still night? My arms dangle; the very tips of my fingers brush against something. Sharp mosaic tiles flit between my digits as I try to work out what is beneath me. If I can somehow free myself, I'd want to have some idea of what I'm going to land on. I know the only way I can begin to make sense of this new reality is by opening my eyes.

But it hurts to do so. A crust has dried over the lids, matting my eyelashes together. It reminds me of a recurring childhood nightmare. My head would close up, every orifice sealing up tight. I'd press my fingers into my ears, the world a numb echo. I could feel myself digging out wax. It was thick and tacky. But no matter how ravenously I excavated, how deep I went, I could never scrape enough of the muck away to open my ear canals. So I'd turn my attention to my mouth. My teeth were ground shut. The hinge of my jaw locked. I'd try to pry my waxy fingers between the incisors, my fingernails would press against the enamel, but nothing more. I'd scratch and scrape, but entry was denied. On the odd occasion I managed to get my bloodied fingers between the upper and lower plates, any attempt to pull them apart was impossible. I'd make a small gap, desperate to breathe, but fearful of sticking my tongue out in case my hold weakened and I'd clamp down, my teeth sawing through it in an accidental act of self-mutilation.

But none of that surpassed the feeling of having my eyes gummed shut and being unable to do anything about it. With chipped fingernails, I tried to scratch enough of the crust away so I could catch a glimmer of light through the barrier. But every time I made a hole, my eyelashes would weave together tighter and tighter, closing the gap so that nothing but pulsing crimson remained.

Yet this isn't my dream.

I can hear people breathing heavily. Someone behind me splutters and curses. Is that Dion? Pulling my hands up to my face is agony. I paw at my eyes, desperate to not suffer a similar fate to that of my nightmare. I can feel dried balls of scab and pus press against my eyes, but slowly, I manage to open them.

It takes a few seconds for me to adjust to my unusual position. My mind tries to soften the blow by suggesting I am suspended over a still, shimmering lake, moonlight and stars casting raindrop ripples on the surface. They twinkle and dazzle. But as I blink faster and start to focus, I see that it isn't water, but glass: hundreds and thousands of broken pieces. At its centre, an island protrudes from the starlit ocean. The peninsula of this uncharted land mass is Charlie's head; his open eyes are low-hanging twin moons completing the macabre nocturnal scene.

His face is slashed from brow to chin. In places, fruit rind skin is peeled back, exposing the muscle and bone beneath. He lies there, his back twinkling as light catches the shards of glass jutting out from his body, exactly how he looked in his open grave back at the pub. But this time he is not buried within a machine, rather splayed on the ground outside. The asphalt of an English country lane. The only light I can see slicing through the gloom is being cast out from a solitary headlight. It is the moon and it is the sun.

I try to swallow but the restraint is digging into my throat. I wrap my hands around the strap and push myself back. The taut seatbelt cuts into my fingers. I manage to take a deep breath before I can no longer support my weight and I fall back into its pinching caress. I look directly beneath me and see a puddle of blood. There in the middle is a solitary finger, the prow of a shipwreck in the bloodied brine, a gold sovereign ring still around it. It points up at me, accusingly, picking out the guilty party from a line-up of one.

I look to my left and there he is. Paul. The roof provided scant protection and has been effortlessly crushed. The thing that was once human has been compressed between seat and metal. His head has snapped forward, resting in a crumpled void between the roof and the edge of what's left of the windscreen. I can see his spine, the skull having been knocked clean from its resting place. His right arm is broken so badly that when the wind blows, it nudges it according to its own whim. An arm bone protrudes through the palm of his hand; as the breeze relinquishes its claim, his hand is set free and it swings down, the bone scraping and scratching against the dashboard, the first three marks of a crude five-bar gate etched into the plastic.

From outside, I can hear the crunch of glass. From my periphery, I see a pair of boots crossing past my window to the front of the minibus. "Hello?" I mumble through broken teeth. "Who's there?"

The feet come to a halt by Charlie. The squeak of glass grazing against the road makes me wince. Someone crouches down, flicking the tails of their trench coat out behind them. A hand holding a cigarette goes to touch Charlie's ripped-open face but stops at the last moment. A finger traces down the split channel of skin, from the temple, down the cheek, and ending by his Adam's apple. A head ducks down, so close to Charlie's that it must surely feel the steam escaping from his wounds. "Hello down there."

"S-S-Simon?"

He gives me a weak salute. "This is quite the mess you've caused, huh?"

"Wh-what's going on?"

"I'd say it's pretty obvious, isn't it? Someone had one too many, lost control, and left... this." Simon blows out a pall of smoke over Charlie's face, the ends of ragged strips of flensed skin forming a bridge from man to road. Simon's head disappears from view as he stands up; I can see his feet turn on the spot, eliciting another squeal of tormented glass from the sole of his shoe. He walks slowly from where Charlie lies, having been ejected from the back seat of the minibus and through the windscreen. His sudden and violent departure has left a greasy trail down the crumpled bonnet, tufts of clothing and meat revealing the flightpath to his final resting place.

I lift myself again so I can take in another breath. This one pains me. I cough, and blood splatters over the rear-view mirror that lets me look inside the wreckage. Jen is squirming in her window seat trying to wake Neil, who hangs from his seatbelt. He's not moving, and every time she shakes him, his head wobbles in time with her growing desperation. His eyes are balls of sandblasted glass; blood is smeared beneath his nose, giving him a red moustache.

I can hear Dion again. "Mattie, wake up." From where I'm hanging, I can only just make them out. They're free of their seatbelts at least – her body is resting on his lap, the pair having taken refuge in a back corner of the van. He's stroking her hair; she twitches as if trapped in a bad dream. Another crunch of glass to my side, and I turn to see Simon making his way towards the pair.

"Poor Matilda, she doesn't sound too good," he says.

I squirm and try to wriggle free from my captivity. I press my thumb against the release button, trying, hoping, that it'll pop and deliver me to the floor. It'll be a jolt of an arrival, but at least then I can try to help.

"Hang on. Gimme a minute," I mumble. I fiddle with the mechanism, but it's not budging.

Dion is crying now. He's saying something but I can't make out the words. I see him cradling her head – her arms are limp and move in time with his rocking. The footsteps from outside stop, and Simon ducks his head in through a broken window. "I'm no doctor, but I don't think she's got long. Poor Matilda."

"Leave her alone. It's me you want, isn't it? I'm the one who's fucked it all up. I should be the one about to breathe my last."

"It doesn't work like that, I'm afraid. You wanted to know what happened… here you go. Is it better, or worse?"

"What?"

"Is it better or worse than you expected?"

"I… I don't know. I don't think anything can be worse than this."

Simon shakes his head. "You'd think by now, you would have learned."

"What?"

"That things can always be worse."

Dion screams from the rear of the mangled minibus. He pulls Matilda's body closer to him, smoothing her hair down, his fingers catching in the knots.

Simon clicks his fingers. "It's time for her to go."

Nine

The pub swims back into view, a wretched transition which makes me feel nauseous. Simon is standing in the doorway. "Such a shame."

I hear the front door click open. Mattie is pulling the handle as Dion looks on from the bar, holding a wine glass by its delicate stem. I vault over the top of the bar, nearly kicking him in the head in the process. As Mattie goes to step into the rushing void, I slam the door shut, pressing myself against it, barring her exit. "On no you don't. You're not going anywhere."

"It's not going to work," says Simon.

"It's my choice, isn't it? I choose for her *not* to go. There. Decision made."

"If it were that simple, do you think I would be here? You think that all of this would simply disappear? No. The time for you to choose the outcome is over. You're done. It's out of my hands now, I'm afraid."

I turn the key in the lock and pocket it. "What do you mean? What part do you play in all of this?"

"I told you. I'm a debt collector."

"And what debt are you collecting, exactly?"

Simon jabs a dirty finger at each of us, Charlie included. "All. Of. You."

"No. I don't care. I'm not going to let this happen."

Simon laughs. "You really don't get this at all, do you?"

Before I can answer, something smashes behind me. I turn to see that Mattie has clambered onto the upholstered bench that rests against the wall by the broken window. She's punching the frame, trying to make a bigger hole. I bound over to her, grabbing hold of her leg just as she wraps her fingers around the outside edge of the windowsill, trying to pull herself through. "No, come on, Mattie. Not like this. Fight. You don't have to go if you don't want to."

"Just bloody well leave her," Dion slurs from the bar. He tips the last of the wine into his mouth and reaches for the bottle; I can see him trying to work out which one is real and which are just mirages.

There isn't much to Mattie, but she's got the strength of a dog on a lead chasing a ball. I manage to wrap my hands round her waist, but I can't get any leverage. With her hands outside, she's able to anchor herself and resist my attempt to haul her back in. "Come on, Mattie, please. Give me a chance." She continues to struggle. "Let me try to make this right."

For a fraction of a second, she stops. I seize the opportunity and climb on her back, trying to weigh her down. No sooner have I managed to straddle her shoulders than she's trying to push me off and climb through the window again. Squeezing my legs together, I reach through the broken pane and try to pry her bloodied fingers from the sill.

"Why don't you just do the decent thing and let her go?" Dion shouts, pouring more wine onto the floor than into his trembling glass. "If it's her time, like the chap over there says, then just bloody well leave her. It's the right thing to do."

No. I'm not having that. I need to work out what's happening. If I fucked up, and it wouldn't be the first time, then I want a shot at sorting it out. And the only way I can salvage anything from this wreck is to make sure that everyone who is still alive stays that way.

Her fingers are slick with blood and, one-by-one, I manage to pull them free. With one hand removed, I shove her arm down by the side of her body and wrench her other hand free. As soon as the connection to the outside world is broken, she starts to struggle and howl. Dion tuts and walks over. "Come on, you, get off her," he tells me.

"I ain't getting off her until she's sat at the bar."

He sighs. "Fine. Mattie, come on, let's go and get a drink. On me."

Like a scolded animal, Mattie goes limp and slips between my legs. Dion escorts her back to a stool and shoves her wine under her nose. She takes the glass, but her eyes are on me. I pick up Paul's table and try to barricade the window as best I can. It's not going to hold for long, but it should buy me enough time if any of them make another dash for it.

I move back behind the bar and hand them a full bottle of wine. "On the house."

Dion's glare eases and he fills the glasses to the rim, running a finger down a trickle spilling from the lip. "Not a bad drop, if a little tart." I go to take the bottle from him, but Mattie starts to scrabble on her seat. Dion puts an arm around her.

"It's okay, shh."

"What's the matter with her? I just fucking saved her, didn't I?"

"She's scared."

"We all should be. There are monsters out there!" I point to the door.

"Well there's one in here, too!" Dion yells back. We stare at each other, he balls his fists and begins to size me up. Working out if he can take me down in one punch, or if he's going to need help. I've got the benefit of being behind the bar – could always pelt him with some empty glasses, clock him round the head with a bottle off the optics if needs be. We're locked in the shittest standoff; there's no tumbleweed, no countdown from a ticking pocket watch. Just two scared people trying to protect the others, when all we're really doing is making the situation worse.

Jen breaks the silence. "What do you mean, *monsters?*"

"I dunno for sure what's out there, but there's something waiting for us. We're not where we should be, and wherever we are, we're not meant to be here. It's like we're trapped in this bubble that we can't escape from and we're falling. But it's night and I can't see where we are, but I can hear voices. Animals, people, they're trapped here too, or they're a part of this, I don't know. I haven't a fucking clue what's happening, except whatever *this* is, it killed Paul, Charlie and—"

"Go on." Jen takes a sip of her drink. "You can say his name."

"And Neil."

Simon claps his hands. "Not too bad, except for one small detail."

"Which is?"

"This place didn't kill them."

"Silly me, Charlie must've propelled *himself* through the window."

"You asked me to show you what happened, so I did, yet you still refuse to accept the truth."

"Truth? What truth? Three people are fucking dead tonight, and all because they went out there into… *that*."

"My point remains, the night didn't kill these people, did it?" Simon points at me. "You did."

"What does he mean?" Dion perks up, swaying on the stool.

Whether it was down to pride, embarrassment, or fear of punishment, it took me years before I could raise my hand and accept the blame for things, and it's important that you own your mistakes. You can't go through life and celebrate your achievements if you can't admit when you've ballsed up. And this is as big as it gets. "There was a crash as we came back from the match. I must've had too much to drink. I don't even know how we got here… but I've seen it. The aftermath of it, I mean. When I came to, I thought this place was real, but it's not. I don't know what it is, or where we are, but we are all in serious trouble."

"Because of you?" Dion sets his glass down.

"Yep, and before you get all funny with me, yes, I'm sorry. I wish I could go back in time and stop it all, but—"

"Life doesn't work that way," Simon chips in.

"Quite. So I need to work out how to get us all out of this place. There's got to be a way. I just know that if anyone goes out there, then they're dead. Gone. No chance of coming back."

"You've still not said much about what you *have* seen," Jen says, folding her arms.

"I only saw flashes. There's nothing out there. Sod all. But this place is falling." I put a hand on the wall and I can feel it. "Even now, it's slower than before, but we're still going down. I could hear this droning sound, it's everywhere, but before Paul went out there it split up, into voices, not just people, but animals too."

"What are the voices saying?" Jen asks.

"That we… that we belong to them."

"And who are *they*?" Dion chips in.

"I don't know! All I saw when Paul left was him waiting outside and then he was just gone. It was like the blackness just took him, before it threw him against the wall. No doubt whatever did that also threw Charlie through the window."

"I wouldn't say that was wholly accurate. Would you?" Simon takes a drag.

"Fine. Yes, that was me. Okay? I took my eye off the road for a few seconds, must've hit something. Charlie wasn't wearing his seatbelt and… he's gone. They're all gone. It's why I couldn't let you go, Mattie."

She looks at me, holding the base of her wine glass and supping from the top. Once she has made a gap, she picks the glass up. "But it's my time," she says, looking across to Simon, "isn't it? I mean, it feels like it is." Silence swaddles us. From the radio, Ben E. King sings the chorus to *Stand by Me*. Mattie breaks the quiet. "I don't belong here, do I?"

"Where do you belong?" Simon asks.

Mattie looks across to the barricaded window. "Out there. With them. I can hear the voices now, too. They're so clear. But there's so many of them. They talk over each other, but I can hear every word they say. So keen to meet me. To meet all of us." She looks across to Jen. "I can hear him, you know."

"Who?" Jen clutches her glass.

"Neil. He's talking to me right now, along with the rest of them. Paul and Charlie, too. They're all a part of the choir, they always will be." Mattie's hand shoots out and grabs Jen's arm. "All we have to do is accept that it's our time. Walk out of that door. They're waiting for us there. Neil is waiting for you there. Come on, why don't we go? I'm not supposed to be here anymore, none of us are, so let's go to a place where we all belong."

I pull Jen free from Mattie's clutches. "We're not just going to give up and walk out there. We have to find a way out of this, it's got to be possible. There has to be a way."

Simon shouts. "This isn't a game, you know! You aren't going to be able to face what's out there and beat it. There is no happy ending to this little adventure. One way or another, you are going to die. All that matters now is who you take with you. It's all this has ever been about."

I step out from behind the bar, grabbing half-stools and chairs, piling them up in front of the door. As I do so, everyone just looks at me as if I'm doing something they don't understand. "No. I'm not having that. There's always a way."

From outside there is a rumbling, which grows into a roar. The volume increases until it is shaking the horse brasses nailed to the walls. Charlie's body is jostled free from his temporary tomb and he smacks into the ground, thick, lumpy black blood oozing from his mouth and the gouges in his face. Something hits the roof of the pub. Once. Twice. Three times. The walls are shaking. Even though the entire bar is being buffeted, the four of them drink on.

I cling onto the brass rail that runs along the front of the bar, trying to stay on my feet. The crappy mountain of furniture I've formed by the door falls apart, an avalanche of upholstered fixtures and fittings. The tremors begin to subside as the roar fades away. "I think you're forgetting one tiny little detail in all of this," Simon says.

"Which is?" I can feel my heart slamming in my chest.

"The choice you think you've been given is not the one you've been asked to make."

Ten

This is beginning to swamp me. Too many things, most of them out of my hands and completely unfathomable. I need to try and get some semblance of control back. Deal with the things that I can influence, which is easier said than done when there's something pressing against the walls outside. Dust puffs out from the joins between the mortar, and from corners long since abandoned to cleaning. The card holders, clinging onto their savoury snacks, have fallen off the wall. There's no point putting them back up; they'll only end up back on the floor.

I can't let myself become side-tracked by the little stuff. I need to triage what I've got to deal with, starting with the obvious. Since trying to get out of the window, Mattie has settled down and doesn't look like she's going anywhere – for now, at least. Simon waves at the empty glasses strewn on the bar. "Another round, if you please."

"Gimme a minute." He's the last of my concerns. Although he's a rogue element and I need to keep an eye on him, my priority right now is to focus on the things I can do, the things that are in my control. I need to shut it all out and remember what little plans I have. I need to save those who are left, and the best way I have of doing that is to try and make this place as safe as possible. The windows in the bar are all hidden behind curtains; it's muffling the sound of those bloody voices, but it ain't brilliant. The gaping hole in the window is as blocked as I can manage. If I had the luxury of time I'm sure I could find something to do a better job, but there are more pressing concerns. Throughout the entire night, I've not checked the rest of the pub. Could there be something there that might offer a way out of this?

I barge past Simon, who's holding out a tenner. Behind him is a door that leads to a small hallway and the toilets. There's a window in that corridor that faces out to the back of the building. You'd only be able to look through if you climbed over a neighbouring fence, but as neither neighbour nor fence exist here, I need to check what does. One simple aim right now: secure the perimeter.

The door to the corridor is heavy, one of those that's been built to contain a fire; as I pull on it, it feels like there's an inferno building behind me. Tension. Fear. Distrust. Each of these are the fuel and kindling. It would only take one spark, one more revelation of regret, one more of us to get sent outside, and the bonfire I've built in this place with my actions would ignite the whole fucking lot. Then the only thing left would be to sit back and watch it burn.

Letting the door close slowly behind me, I notice the change in temperature out here. The window isn't open, but it's markedly cooler. The voices are louder too, their words echoing up and down the corridor. I grab hold of the curtain hems and jerk them closed – this dulls their intensity but makes the building shake and shudder even more. I can hear bricks grinding against each other like the teeth from my nightmare, loosening the mortar and making cracks appear. The light from above is sucked out through the gaps and consumed by the darkness. We're a galaxy of light being pulled into a black hole. Stripped down to our base parts and added to the invisible mass out there.

I push the door to the Gents, but nothing happens – same with the Ladies. They're nothing but room dressing. These chambers aren't important. They're just there to keep us in.

The lightbulbs flicker and fail for a few seconds, followed by a sudden jolt, then a resettling of the ground beneath me. Fizzing back on, light floods the small corridor and I feel that we're no longer moving. We've hit rock bottom, and with nothing left out here to deal with, I try my best to ignore the sound of the building being crushed and push open the door to the bar.

I half-expect to return and find no-one there, the pub a Marie Celeste left drifting in this unforgiving world. But the survivors are exactly where I left them. Simon jiggles his empty glass at me. "Happy now?"

"Fine, what are you having?"

"Same again, a pint of the black stuff. Anyone else want one?"

Dion points to the wine bottle. "Absolutely fine over here, thank you, good sir."

"I'll have another G&T, please," Jen chips in.

I get her drink sorted first, knowing that Simon's will take time. Plus, it means he has to wait, something he acknowledges with a smile. "While you're pouring mine, why don't I tell you what I know?"

"Deal." I set down Jen's tonic water and angle Simon's fresh glass under the spout. "Well? I'm waiting."

He retrieves another cigarette from the packet, sparking it into life before he starts. "There's a reason people are afraid of the dark, you know." He points to the haphazard barricade I've erected. "There's more than just that waiting out there for you… for us. Since time began, the darkness has always been there. It is everlasting, no matter what happens – regardless of how many lives begin and end, the night is eternal. And in there lurks not monsters, but the remnants of that life, in a world just beyond ours. Sometimes, when there's a crack between our realities, the mass of unlife can see in, and likewise, we're able to look right back. That's where the monsters that plague your nightmares come from. The things that go bump in the night."

My hand shakes as he speaks. "How did—"

"I know more than you'd think. You're struggling to deal with the fact that what you're facing here is not something you can see, touch, or run from. It is everywhere, it is nowhere. But it is inexorable and to think you can hide or even fight it, is ridiculous to the point of absurdity. All you are, in this place, is food."

"Paul and the others, they got eaten?"

"In a fashion. The night consumes energy from all living things, but in particular, the energy that explodes from us all at the point of death. And trust me, it would not pass up the opportunity of a tasty morsel" – he looks around the room – "or half a dozen." Simon taps his ash into the ashtray. "This place is a sliver of skin away from the one you know." He chops at the air. "Here in this world, you're serving me a drink," he says, pointing at the floor between us, "whilst in your world, you're currently bleeding internally, a lung punctured, your other organs squeezed and battered. As you or your associates leave that world, you also leave this one, but not before your essence is devoured and added to the conglomeration of energy that it has amassed since the universe began."

With the Guinness having reached its mark, I rest it on the plastic shelf beneath the tap. "This is bollocks, there's no heaven or hell."

"Did I say there was?"

"Well… no, but—"

"Whether you die in your bed at a hundred years old, or you bleed to death hanging upside down in a car crash that you caused, the end result is the same."

"Which is?"

Simon stubs out the cigarette. "You disappear into nothingness. All of you. None of you are spared this fate."

"Then what's the fucking point in all of this? Is it some kind of sick game?"

"On the contrary, it's something that most people don't get."

"And that is? Come on, just spit it out, will you?"

"Why do you think you're reminiscing so much tonight? Isn't that a little peculiar, or do you often spend your evenings running through every little mistake you made, every event that left a mark?"

"I don't get it…"

Simon leans over the bar. "Shouldn't you top that off?" I pick up the glass and push the tap handle backwards; the dark liquid hits the blackness in the glass sending plumes of brown wake rushing towards the base. "The gap between this world and yours has created a bridge of sorts. You shouldn't be here, but before you expire, before your essence evacuates your vessel, you've been afforded a luxury that most don't get. A chance to reconcile your life. Your existence. To make peace with everything before it's taken away.

Energy cannot be created or destroyed, so you'll still exist, but not in a form where you're consciously aware of what you once were, here, there."

I flick the tap handle to its stop position and place the glass down on the beer towel. Within, the tumult continues. The brown waves struggle for survival, but from the bottom to the top, it is settling. Becoming one with the blackness. "I don't want to die."

"Most people don't. I know I didn't."

"How did you end up doing this?"

He chuckles. "Luck. Good or bad, I couldn't tell you. But from time to time, this place requires people like *me* to help guide people like *you* that get stuck in this limbo. I often joke to myself that I'm less of a debt collector and more of a toilet brush, here to help scrape off the people that cling on doggedly to the bowl. Those who don't want to let go. Some become trapped within the constructs of this world, surviving within a chamber of light for years on end, keeping the night at bay. In your world, they live only in a coma, whilst here they are slowly driven mad by the inexorable knowledge that they're going to die. The only way they can survive here for so long is to shut out the darkness, but it is a forlorn hope, and can only end one way."

"But what about everyone else tonight? Why me and not them?"

"Guilt. You were the one who put them here. The only one that was consciously aware – albeit in some small way – of what happened. They're here because you are, not the other way round. You're the sun in this room, everyone else is being pulled towards you – and sooner or later, like Paul, Charlie, and Neil, they're going to get torn apart. In this place, a lot like this building, they're just approximations of their complete selves. Enough is created for them to play their part, nothing else. They don't get to choose, only you. Now," he says, picking up the glass, the liquid within having settled to the colour of tar, "how about a toast?"

"I don't have a drink," I mumble.

"Well, best go and get one then, hadn't you! What better time is there to drink than at the end of everything you've ever known?"

I open the fridge behind me and retrieve a bottle of Newcastle Brown. Simon holds his pint towards the four of us. "To you all." One-by-one, the others reciprocate. Dion clinks his glass against Simon's, Mattie does likewise. Jen holds hers up reluctantly, and they all look at me. "Fine." I knock the top of the bottle against their drinks. "Cheers."

Simon lowers his glass and holds it out. As it sits in my eyeline I see something stir within the liquid. At first I think it's just the final throes of the Guinness settling, but then I see that the liquid is not moving from top to bottom, but horizontally. The liquid is spinning slowly around the glass, with each rotation it picks up speed. Simon points the glass towards Mattie, making the movement stop. From within the glass, I can hear voices. Small. Distant. Solemn. They merge into one singular chorus: "You belong to us," before their words bleed into the veins of the sonorous thrum outside, now a concrete wall of noise.

There's no time to react, no time to do anything but watch, as the blackness within the glass erupts into Mattie's face. In a moment, Simon's glass is entirely emptied, and the thick tar pulses and oozes into Mattie's mouth, ears, and eyes. It slips up her nostrils, gloopy tendrils crawling around her cheeks and slipping into her ears, taking advantage of any means it can to invade her. Throughout this, she does nothing to fight it off. Nothing to repel this interloper. Everyone, me included, just stands there like statues and watch as it coats her entire head. It's shiny, the light from above reflecting off its surface. But there's a hissing sound too, water on a high stove, bubbling away, evaporating into nothingness. As it settles, it seeps into her pores, until her skin is visible once more, dulled with a grey sheen. Wispy strands of infection swim across the whites of her eyes. Her skin writhes as the ink courses through her veins, multiplying and expanding throughout her body.

Then Mattie's eyes clear and her body ceases rippling with subdermal movement. "Mattie, are you okay?" I ask. That dumb question again. In reply, she falls from her stool, smacking into the floor. I lean over the bar and see thick black lines trickling from her ears and nose. I'm given no respite as the drone outside continues to rise, increasing the crushing pressure on the building. The eggshell-brickwork can take no more and begins to crack. The light above Charlie flares, adding an ear-piercing screech that only ends when the bulb explodes and delivers that part of the room into darkness. My solitary, selfish hope is that it'll act as a proper shroud to cover poor Charlie, but his gouged head and hands still poke out of the gloom. His fingers have pulled into claws, their nails dug into the carpet as if in anticipation of what is about to happen next.

With the protective barrier of light gone, this rotten vessel we're trapped in now resting on the bed of this damned place, the night seizes the opportunity. The darkness rushes in from the cracks in the shattered window, a pyroclastic cloud of gloom pouring over the broken furniture, hiding it beneath its ebony cloak. From the void, the droning breaks into a chorus of excited shouts and yips. The night can sense that it has a foothold in here with us now. It knows that our end is nigh.

The blackness laps over Charlie's feet, slowly covering him in a midnight shroud. Charlie's eyes begin to roll up inside his skull. Mid-transition, they leer at me as fat black fingers inch out from the freshly claimed territory, wrapping over his shoulders slowly, taking care to ensure they can gain purchase over their prize.

Slowly, the corpse is concealed within the shadows. As his shoulders disappear into the murk, his eyes manage one final look of accusation at me before he's immersed entirely. With his body submerged by the encroaching blackness, the din outside begins to subside, though I can still feel we're being gripped tightly. I round on Simon. "What the hell was that in your glass?"

"It was her time to go. I've told you already, you can't stop it, no matter how hard you try. If you resist – like you did earlier – it *will* just find another way. That's what it does. It cannot be denied."

"How do I stop it? It's affected by the light, yeah? I can get it with light. Keep us safe with it, perhaps I can get a fire going?"

Simon shakes his head. "Through the cracks between the light, night will find a way and let the darkness in. Do you honestly believe they won't repeat what they just did to get you all? This is pointless. Just give in. There's nothing left for you now, no hope. Nothing. Let it have you. Let it have you all."

The part of the pub which has been freshly annexed by the outside has calmed down. It pulses slowly, but the fact that it's now in here with us – a matter of feet away – means that my options are diminishing. I can still get to the front door – just – but for how long?

Back to the practical: I know what I'm going to find when I get there, but I have to check on Mattie, mainly because no-one else is going to bother. Dion's eyes have welled up, but he's still studying the contents of his glass as if he's divining for gold. Thing is, I'm worried about checking on her. I'm scared of what's coming out of her nose and mouth. From a distance it looks like the tar that suffocated her, but as I kneel over her, I'm relieved to see that it's just blood.

Just. Blood.

My entire life is teetering on the edge of oblivion right now, and the only thing I've got chalked up in the win column is that it's *only* a person's life force bubbling out of their face and not some nightmarish gloop formed from a pint of Guinness. "Mattie," I whisper, as if she's sleeping. It's painfully clear from the way she's lying here – and the amount of blood her head is resting in – that she's already gone. Another taken by the night.

But that's not the whole story, is it? These people are only here because of me, and I'm letting them go, one-by-one. Who's next? Does it even matter? Simon pipes up. "It's Dion."

"What?"

"The next person to go. I know you're wondering."

I think back to when I woke up trapped in the minibus, Paul's body – like the one here – squashed down into his chair, Charlie sprawled on the floor outside, Neil's neck broken from the impact. But then

I remember beyond the obvious. "Hang on, Dion was sitting up in the minibus."

"So?"

"It means he's alive and well, at least well enough to have let Mattie out of her seat belt, after himself of course, and to have stayed with her. As… she was… you know."

"Dying."

"Yeah."

Simon places the empty glass on the side. "And? Why does that matter?"

"If he's okay enough to have done that, he can get out of the wreckage. Call for help."

"I can only tell you what I know, which is that Dion is next."

"How do you know?"

Simon points to the window. "Because it told me."

"But I thought I was the one with the choice?"

"You are. But if you bothered to listen to what I've been trying to tell you, the choice you get to make it not the one you think it is. You're not choosing between these people. Your choice is between them and you."

"I don't believe you, this is bullshit."

Simon clicks his fingers. "Fine."

Eleven

My guts lurch as I shift from standing in the bar to upside-down suspension once more. The noise from behind me is Dion shouting. I can see him punching the seat cushions even as he holds Mattie's limp body against his own, losing his grip with each blow until finally she slips free and melts into the floor, no tension left in her. With her body no longer a concern, he uses both fists to pummel the padded seats.

"Dion!" I have to shout so he can hear me over his grief. He's lost in his own hell; nothing can reach him. All lines of communication are down. A tsunami of loss has swept in and broken every levee he has. "Dion!"

He stops mid-punch, his eyes heavy rain clouds, misted and indistinct. "What?"

"We have to get out of here."

"Mattie... she's gone." He scoops up her body and holds it out to me, thinking I have the power to save her. But that ship has long since sailed and the guilt threatens to drown me in its undertow. "She's bloody gone."

"I know, but if we don't get out of here right fucking now, then we're going to go, too."

Dion shrugs. "So what? I don't care anymore."

"Come on, please. I'm hurt pretty bad, I can't get out. You need to get over here and help me out. Please."

"Why? What's the point?"

"BECAUSE I DON'T WANT TO FUCKING DIE! IS THAT OKAY WITH YOU?"

The words hit him, but they don't seem to sink in. Those barriers of his are rebuilding; they'll go up taller than they ever were, thicker. They have to. Not only do they have to keep out everything from before, but now they have to contend with this, too. He takes a big sniff, one that sucks everything up. From outside, I hear footsteps walking back towards me. They stop, and Simon ducks down. "How is that rescue plan of yours working out?"

"Please, Simon, come on. Help me. Help them."

He ignores me and sinks to all fours. In the corner of his mouth is the dying butt of a cigarette. Blowing the smoke into my face, he flicks the smouldering stick behind him into the undergrowth. "You want me to intervene?"

"Yes, come on!"

"I mean… I *could*. Should I?"

"If not for me, for the others, they shouldn't have to pay for my mistake. Please."

"Okay. I'll intervene, if you insist."

"Thank you, if you could—" The words die in my mouth as I peer out at the horizon. Past Charlie's pulped body, past the ocean of glass, and into the blackness of night. There, blue strobes whirl and slice through the fog and the gloom. Carried on the breeze are the stirrings of a siren. I crane my head as far back as I can, calling out to Dion and Jen. "Just hold on, okay, help is on the way. Someone must've phoned it in." I look at Simon. "Thank you."

Simon leans into the smashed vehicle, his hands pressing against the broken glass. He's level with me now; I get another whiff of his fusty aroma. He's so close to me that I can't see what he's doing. "It's no good, I don't think my seat belt can come loose, let them cut me out." But I don't feel any pressure on the band that holds me in place. "Simon?"

He reappears then, shuffling back out the way he came in. Free of the wreck, he stays kneeling, dusting himself off. "That's not my doing." He holds out a closed fist to me. "This is."

"What is it?" My brain is running beyond capacity now, the blood pooling in the top of my body. My fingers wrap around his, fumbling to open his hand up.

Simon turns his head. "What's that smell?"

I've been so preoccupied with what I can see and hear that the smells of the minibus have become secondary. Past the tang of blood and Simon's mustiness, there's something else. I pry his fist open. No. He *lets* me reveal what he's holding, just as the pang of recognition hits. "Petrol," I mumble. And there it is. Sat in the middle of his palm. My lighter. Before I can snatch it, he withdraws from the broken window, footsteps signalling his path to the edge of the narrow country lane. As he leaves, I see the gasoline tide flow towards me. It shimmers from the hue of the moon above, clouds having parted to allow it look down upon us. Its dark grey craters form a face which shows no compassion for our fate. Simon squats down at the side of the road; his clothing blends into the gloaming. He cocks his head towards the blue lights which flare in the distance. "I'm sorry to say, I don't think they're going to get here in time."

"No, please. Not like this."

He places his thumb on the lid and rocks it to the side. "Everyone dies. Everyone. Not everyone gets given a choice, but you did, and what did you do with that precious gift? You chose to waste it. Being cast into that world was not damnation, but a chance at others' salvation. Yet, with every choice you made, you damned these people. You could've saved them, all of them, but you chose not to. So now they all have to pay for your mistake." He rolls the wheel; sparks fly but they do not catch light. "It's funny."

"What?"

"In order to deliver you to the darkness, I have to let the light in." Simon thumbs the wheel again and a flame blooms into life. He lowers the lighter down over the expanding lake of petrol. Its reflection dances over the surface, foretelling what will happen when it is ignited.

I hold my hand out and scream.

"NO! STOP!"

Twelve

Dion and Jen are looking at me. Simon, too. We're back in the pub again, but it's changed. The lights have dimmed; it seems as if we've been buried for centuries and only just been uncovered. That's our marker, isn't it? That's the real yardstick of progress. But we get so fucking bogged down in the trivialities of day-to-day life that more often than not, we fail to see. To truly see. To appreciate the times when you manage to achieve what you've strived and longed for. Life is evolution. Whether it's something as grand as adaptation by an entire species, or as small as taking back control of your own fate, we evolve. We must. What else is there? What use would it be for us to dwell in the depths of despair if, when we had climbed back up to the light, we did not revel in that moment?

I never imagined I would experience such a short time being alive. So narrow a window. But I see it now. I see why I resisted in this place for so long. *Life is so unfair.* Why me? Why should I give myself up so that others may live? Why should I be the one who has to help others, when often that was not afforded to me? We all truly suffer in silence. All of us are utterly alone; the only person who will ever know what you have gone through, or what you are truly capable of, is you. Whilst the company of others should be sought, experiences shared and fortune split, when we lie on the altar at the end of our lives, we are shorn of everything and everyone.

You take nothing and no-one with you. For you are going somewhere that requires neither of these. We are born from the darkness – and in death are returned to it.

That's all it is, this life. A string pinned out from one point in time to another. Sometimes that string frays, at times it breaks and needs to be knotted back together again. But one day, it will end. We are swallowed up by the universe once more, our essence redistributed out to the cosmos. It doesn't matter if you missed out on your birthday cake, or if you silently called out for everything to end in your bed. Only you know of that pain. And with your passing, it too shall disappear.

I see that now. I get it.

"Are you ready?" Simon asks.

His coat is writhing, the material now made from the same shadows that have seeped into our broken sanctuary. The only things of him that are solid are his head and hands. Wisps of shade reach out from this cloud of blackness, trying to find something to latch onto. And that's all we do. We spend our lives searching for people we can tolerate and things we enjoy, but all we are left with is thin air. "Will it hurt?" I ask.

"Yes. More than you've ever known."

But that doesn't bother me. What is a singular moment of excruciating agony compared to an infinity of existence? From the dawn of time to its end, that moment would not even be something that could be registered.

I look at the playing cards on the bar. Tendrils of black have sprouted from the spades and clubs, charred fronds of seaweed caught in an invisible tide. The night has taken root here now – there is no escape from it.

I open the flap of the bar and walk towards the door. Simon is waiting for me there, as Dion and Jen pivot on their stools and look on. I pass Mattie and see that in the shadows of her body, in the dried puddles of blood, the blackness has taken residence there too. Gaunt wraiths flicker from her open mouth as black fire rakes up and down the infected veins in her arm. Her eyes regard me as if I am nothing, knowing that soon, I will be.

I unbolt the door and rest my hand on the latch. It's then that I remember the name of that damn Elton John song that was playing when I came to in this place. "Sacrifice."

Simon nods and retrieves his last cigarette, discarding the crumpled box onto the floor. It lands upside-down, a sick parody of my final resting place. I pull my lighter from my pocket and ignite the cigarette for him. "Much obliged," he says.

I close the lid and hold it out to him. "Something to remember me by." He takes it, rolling it around in his fingers, before letting it be subsumed into the blight of his body.

Simon steps back as I pull the door open. I take a step forward and stand on the edge between the pub and the void beyond. It's everything. It's everywhere. From the highest point to the lowest, there is only blackness. Yet it is not static. It moves. It slips and slides against itself. It roils. It bubbles and simmers. The hubbub of voices settle into their now-familiar refrain. "You belong to us," is now a promise of certainty.

"I choose me, over them. It's my time to go now." I take a single step from everything I've known, everything I've relied upon, and into the unknown. The cavorting maelstrom of motion and sound stops, and from the gloom there's the faintest crack. A mere pinprick of respite from this crushing gloom. A tiny ball of incandescent light. With every step I take, away from the thing I tried to cling onto, the light grows in size. It shines down from the dark heavens onto my face. Behind me, I can feel that the pub has gone. Dion. Jen. Even Simon. They are no longer here in this place, with me, with *it*. In some small way, I feel relieved. That at the end, I was able to do some good. Despite everything, I was able to save someone, even though it meant that I could not be saved myself. And you know what? I'm happy with that now. For I was able to look back over my time and accept the things I once had, and mourn all that I had lost. Acknowledge my own failings and see the person that I was. That's something that most will never get the chance to have. I'm one of the lucky ones.

The light expands, forming a tunnel from it to me, lancing through the nothingness. An iridescent path from here to there. I step on it and stand tall. This is it. This is all I've ever had. Right here. Right now. And it is the most beautiful thing I have ever seen. Any sorrow or disappointment that I possess has evaporated.

I am free.

I walk forwards, and with every step, the light contracts behind me, until it and I are no more, and all there is – all there ever will be – is the night.

Thirteen

Why is it that whenever you need something – I mean, *really* need something – you can never find the damn thing? It's as if objects can sense their impending usage and disappear without a sodding trace. I must've been patting myself down now for the last ten minutes of this midnight jaunt, and I'm still none the wiser as to where the hell my lighter is. Paul appears in my eyeline – unluckily for me, he called shotgun as we left the pub. "What are you looking for?"

I can't even be bothered answering him. He's one of those people that only has to breathe and he annoys me. I'm sure he's a perfectly nice person, but I've got more important things to concern myself with right now, and none of them involve him. I'm tired, and, truth be told, a bit tipsy.

It's got to be here somewhere. With one hand on the steering wheel and half an eye on the road ahead, I try to think back to where I was when I last used it. That's what people always ask at times like this, isn't it? And sure enough, Paul pipes up again. "Where did you see it last?"

Why do we do that? Why do we ask these bloody stupid questions? It's not something that only the Pauls of this world are guilty of, we *all* do it. Why do we *have* to fill the silence with noise? Why can't we just shut the fuck up and enjoy the peace and quiet?

I'm about to answer him when something hiding by the side of the road takes its chance. A few seconds earlier – or later – and our paths never would have crossed. But its ill-timed choice has set us on a collision course. I dab the brakes, hoping it's enough. A crack – audible even through the metal chassis – tells me it wasn't. Paul gives me *that* look. "Did you just—?"

"What was that?" Jen asks from the next row back. Of everyone on board, it had to be *her* who heard the crunch. What with the worry lines etched on the poor cow's face, I'm surprised she can sleep at night. She must spend her entire life on edge.

"It's nothing," I lie, shooting a quick glare across to Paul to lure him into the pact.

"Must've been a rock or something, didn't see anything," he concurs, before resuming his vigil of the world speeding by.

I sit up and grab the wheel with both hands, flex my shoulders, and try to inject an ounce of life back into my flagging body. It's only then I realise the cigarette is still stuck to my lip. I peel it off and tuck it behind my ear, trying to ignore the voice telling me that a smoke will make everything better.

I go to wind the window down before remembering that nothing works on this piece of shit minibus. John has been promising me for the last two years that he'll be fixing this or that. He's had his mate down the garage take care of the MOT on the sly every year since he's had it. Warnings given, promises made, no action taken. The only thing that works on the dashboard is the engine warning light that lives in a permanent state of illumination. Every broken gauge mirrors my physical state, stuck on zero or running cold, and I've lost count of the times I've nearly run out of petrol. Imagined scenarios of trudging back to the last garage, my only company an empty plastic jerry can, and a sole source of light: my Zippo.

Well, it would be, if I could find the fucking thing. Did I lend it to Neil? A quick check in the rear-view mirror shows the rotund mound of man who goes by that name, snoring on Jen's shoulder. His head alone is twice the size of hers, his neck fat easily mistaken for a turtle-neck jumper, the rattling sound of his breathing falling in and out of time with some classical music playing from the only radio station this piece of shit can pick up. The sole source of entertainment in this rust-bucket broke last Christmas, and the one station it can latch onto has been doing its best to gentrify us ever since. Thing is, with this audience – me included – it's about as welcome as those bible junkies on the street peddling their beliefs to anyone who doesn't tell them to fuck off. And, much like them, I've not been able to turn the volume down, because unsurprisingly, that's busted too.

Neil's snoring is fighting (and losing) to stay in sync with some wonderfully uplifting tune called Danse Macabre. He's not complimenting the violins at all, and if I were to say anything, it's highly likely he would wake up and clout me one. Of course, he'd claim to be mucking about, but in my experience, nothing with him is ever done in jest. That bloke wouldn't know a joke if it came up to him, handed over its business card, and delivered its punchline. Neil's got two settings – asleep and petty – and, from what I've seen, nothing in between.

No wonder Jen's permanently on edge. With everything she has to put up with, the last thing she needs to hear is that I've reduced the local rabbit population by one. That somewhere out there, a family of baby bunnies have been orphaned. Reckon they'll give it a day or so, waiting to see if their mum will return, before setting out on their own. Life is a delicate balance at the best of times, and those poor sods have just had their one and only safety blanket ripped away from them. I didn't set out this morning with the intent of murdering mama rabbit – it wasn't on my to-do list. But then, what control do we ever really have? Do you honestly think if I had a choice, I'd be out here ferrying this lot around instead of being tucked up in bed? The answer is a resounding *no*. To labour the point, Dion shouts, "are we nearly there yet?" from the back seats, making Mattie next to him chuckle.

I'm about to give him an earful when Paul asks, "Do you want me to drive?" Not for the first time, either. Ever since we left, he's been on at me. Always with the bloody questions. He could have his own quiz show, except he's got the personality of a muddy puddle.

"I'm fine. We're nearly home now." It'll shut him up for a bit longer, by then we should be on the outskirts of town. Neon lights, piss-heads, perhaps even a few sirens, the general hubbub of kicking-out time on a Thursday night. The sights and sounds of civilisation will be just the tonic, help pin my eyes open and jolt me awake again. Give my brain something more to focus on than two triangles of light strafing down narrow country lanes in the arse-end of the great British countryside.

I can feel my eyes going again. Alcohol makes me tired. Although I've only had a few. It doesn't help that this repetitive little ditty on the radio is doing its best to sing me a lullaby. That's the problem with this sort of music – even when you get the fancy stuff with all that pomp and circumstance, it's just so bloody dull. I can't rely on this to stay awake. The minuscule gap I've managed to make with the window is doing naff-all as well. If I lean over a little bit, I can feel a line of cold down my forehead as if someone's stuck an ice-lolly to it, but it's not enough. If Paul catches me with my neck all crooked like that, he'll make sure I pull over and relegate me to co-pilot. And he'd be fucking unbearable in the driving seat. I've just got to hold on.

"I'm gonna need a piss soon," Charlie pipes up.

"Not long now," I shout back. I've got this, it's simple enough – keep the wheels between the hems of grass and branches a little longer and we'll be there.

I'll tell you what would work: that cigarette. Wake me up a bit. Reckon if I nursed it, I could get ten minutes of guaranteed alertness. Sober me up a bit. Make sure I take my time with it, though, rest it between my fingers on the wheel. Let the glowing cherry add its tiny light to this midnight hour. It'll be a symbol of one of the streetlights outside the pub, a reminder that we'll soon be back. I'd be the hero of the hour – the chauffeur to the rescue once more, carrying the victors back safe and sound. Then just a quick check to make sure the van's locked up before heading inside. Maybe, if I'm lucky, we'll have a lock-in. John will have left a note on the bar: 'Well done, help yourselves to a nightcap. You've done The Dark Horse proud.'

THE THREE BOOKS
by
Paul StJohn Mackintosh

"I've been told that this is the most elegant thing I've ever written. I can't think how such a dark brew of motifs came together to create that effect. But there's unassuaged longing and nostalgia in here, interwoven with the horror, as well as an unflagging drive towards the final consummation. I still feel more for the story's characters, whether love or loathing, than for any others I've created to date. Tragedy, urban legend, Gothic romance, warped fairy tale of New York: it's all there. And of course, most important of all is the seductive allure of writing and of books – and what that can lead some people to do.

You may not like my answer to the mystery of the third book. But I hope you stay to find out."

Paul StJohn Mackintosh

"Paul StJohn Mackintosh is one of those writers who just seems to quietly get on with the business of producing great fiction... it's an excellent showcase for his obvious talents. His writing, his imagination, his ability to lay out a well-paced and intricate story in only 100 pages is a great testament to his skills."

—This is Horror

blackshuckbooks.co.uk/signature

BLACK STAR, BLACK SUN
by
Rich Hawkins

"Black Star, Black Sun *is my tribute to Lovecraft, Ramsey Campbell, and the haunted fields of Somerset, where I seemed to spend much of my childhood. It's a story about going home and finding horror there when something beyond human understanding begins to invade our reality. It encompasses broken dreams, old memories, lost loved ones and a fundamentally hostile universe. It's the last song of a dying world before it falls to the Black Star.*"

Rich Hawkins

————•————

"Black Star, Black Sun *possesses a horror energy of sufficient intensity to make readers sit up straight. A descriptive force that shifts from the raw to the nuanced. A ferocious work of macabre imagination and one for readers of Conrad Williams and Gary McMahon.*"
—Adam Nevill, author of *The Ritual*

"*Reading Hawkins' novella is like sitting in front of a guttering open fire. Its glimmerings captivate, hissing with irrepressible life, and then, just when you're most seduced by its warmth, it spits stinging embers your way. This is incendiary fiction. Read at arms' length.*"
—Gary Fry, author of *Conjure House*

blackshuckbooks.co.uk/signature

DEAD LEAVES

by

Andrew David Barker

"*This book is my love letter to the horror genre. It is about what it means to be a horror fan; about how the genre can nurture an adolescent mind; how it can be a positive force in life.*

This book is set during a time when horror films were vilified in the press and in parliament like never before. It is about how being a fan of so-called 'video nasties' made you, in the eyes of the nation, a freak, a weirdo, or worse, someone who could actually be a danger to society.

This book is partly autobiographical, set in a time when Britain seemed to be a war with itself. It is a working class story about hope. All writers, filmmakers, musicians, painters – artists of any kind –were first inspired to create their own work by the guiding light of another's. The first spark that sets them on their way.

This book is about that spark."

Andrew David Barker

———•———

"*Whilst Thatcher colluded with the tabloids to distract the public... an urban quest for the ultimate video nasty was unfolding, before the forces of media madness and power drunk politicians destroyed the Holy Grail of gore!*"

—Graham Humphreys, painter of *The Evil Dead* poster

blackshuckbooks.co.uk/signature

THE FINITE
by
Kit Power

"The Finite *started as a dream; an image, really, on the edge
of waking. My daughter and I, joining a stream of people
walking past our house. We were marching together, and I saw
that many of those behind us were sick, and struggling, and
then I looked to the horizon and saw the mushroom cloud. I
remember a wave of perfect horror and despair washing over
me; the sure and certain knowledge that our march was doomed,
as were we.*

*The image didn't make it into the story, but the feeling did.
King instructs us to write about what scares us. In* The Finite,
*I wrote about the worst thing I can imagine; my own childhood
nightmare, resurrected and visited on my kid."*

Kit Power

"The Finite *is* Where the Wind Blows *or* Threads *for the
21st century, played out on a tight scale by a father and his
young daughter, which only serves to make it all the more
heartbreaking."*
—Priya Sharma, author of *Ormeshadow*

RICOCHET
by
Tim Dry

"With Ricochet *I wanted to break away from the traditional linear form of storytelling in a novella and instead create a series of seemingly unrelated vignettes. Like the inconsistent chaos of vivid dreams I chose to create stand-alone episodes that vary from being fearful to blackly humorous to the downright bizarre. It's a book that you can dip into at any point but there is an underlying cadence that will carry you along, albeit in a strangely seductive new way.*

Prepare to encounter a diverse collection of characters. Amongst them are gangsters, dead rock stars, psychics, comic strip heroes and villains, asylum inmates, UFOs, occult nazis, parisian ghosts, decaying and depraved royalty and topping the bill a special guest appearance by the Devil himself."

Tim Dry

———•———

Reads like the exquisite lovechild of William Burroughs and Philip K. Dick's fiction, with some Ballard thrown in for good measure. Wonderfully imaginative, darkly satirical - this is a must read!

—Paul Kane, author of *Sleeper(s)* and *Ghosts*

blackshuckbooks.co.uk/signature

ROTH-STEYR
by
Simon Bestwick

"You never know which ideas will stick in your mind, let alone where they'll go. Roth-Steyr *began with an interest in the odd designs and names of early automatic pistols, and the decision to use one of them as a story title. What started out as an oddball short piece became a much longer and darker tale about how easily a familiar world can fall apart, how old convictions vanish or change, and why no one should want to live forever.*

It's also about my obsession with history, in particular the chaotic upheavals that plagued the first half of the twentieth century and that are waking up again. Another 'long dark night of the European soul' feels very close today.

So here's the story of Valerie Varden. And her Roth-Steyr."

Simon Bestwick

———•———

"A slice of pitch-black cosmic pulp, elegant and inventive in all the most emotionally engaging ways."

—Gemma Files, author of *In That Endlessness, Our End*

A DIFFERENT KIND OF LIGHT
by
Simon Bestwick

"When I first read about the Le Mans Disaster, over twenty years ago, I knew there was a story to tell about the newsreel footage of the aftermath – footage so appalling it was never released. A story about how many of us want to see things we aren't supposed to, even when we insist we don't.

What I didn't know was who would tell that story. Last year I finally realised: two lovers who weren't lovers, in a world that was falling apart. So at long last I wrote their story and followed them into a shadow land of old films, grief, obsession and things worse than death.

You only need open this book, and the film will start to play."

Simon Bestwick

———◆———

"Compulsively readable, original and chilling. Simon Bestwick's witty, engaging tone effortlessly and brilliantly amplifies its edge-of-your-seat atmosphere of creeping dread. I'll be sleeping with the lights on."

—Sarah Lotz, author of *The Three, Day Four, The White Road* & *Missing Person*

blackshuckbooks.co.uk/signature

THE INCARNATIONS OF MARIELA PEÑA

by

Steven J Dines

"The Incarnations of Mariela Peña *is unlike anything I have ever written. It started life (pardon the pun) as a zombie tale and very quickly became something else: a story about love and the fictions we tell ourselves.*

During its writing, I felt the ghost of Charles Bukowski looking over my shoulder. I made the conscious decision to not censor either the characters or myself but to write freely and with brutal, sometimes uncomfortable, honesty. I was betrayed by someone I cared deeply for, and like Poet, I had to tell the story, or at least this incarnation of it. A story about how the past refuses to die."

Steven J Dines

---•---

"Call it literary horror, call it psychological horror, call it a journey into the darkness of the soul. It's all here. As intense and compelling a piece of work as I've read in many a year."

—Paul Finch, author of *Kiss of Death* and *Stolen*,
and editor of the *Terror Tales* series.

blackshuckbooks.co.uk/signature

THE DERELICT

by

Neil Williams

"The Derelict *is really a story of two derelicts – the events on the first and their part in the creation of the second.*

With this story I've pretty much nailed my colours to the mast, so to speak. As the tale is intended as a tribute to stories by the likes of William Hope Hodgson or H P Lovecraft (with a passing nod to Coleridge's Ancient Mariner), where some terrible event is related in an unearthed journal or (as is the case here) by a narrator driven to near madness.

The primary influence on the story was the voyage of the Demeter, from Bram Stoker's Dracula, *one of the more compelling episodes of that novel. Here the crew are irrevocably doomed from the moment they set sail. There is never any hope of escape or salvation once the nature of their cargo becomes apparent. This was to be my jumping off point with* The Derelict.

Though I have charted a very different course from the one taken by Stoker, I have tried to remain resolutely true to the spirit of that genre of fiction and the time in which it was set."

Neil Williams

————◆————

"Fans of supernatural terror at sea will love The Derelict. *I certainly did."*

—Stephen Laws, author of *Ferocity* and *Chasm*

blackshuckbooks.co.uk/signature

CPSIA information can be obtained
at www.ICGtesting.com
Printed in the USA
JSHW050243150222
22905JS00001B/16